The Rover Boys at

Arthur M. Win

THE ROVER BOYS
AT COLLEGE

OR

THE RIGHT ROAD AND THE WRONG

BY
ARTHUR M. WINFIELD
(Edward Stratemeyer)
AUTHOR OF THE ROVER BOYS AT SCHOOL, THE
ROVER BOYS ON THE OCEAN, THE PUTNAM HALL SERIES, ETC.

ILLUSTRATED

NEW YORK
GROSSET & DUNLAP
PUBLISHERS
Made in the United States of America

"HOLD IT UP, OR THEY'LL ALL BE KILLED."—*Page* 90.

The Rover Boys at College.

INTRODUCTION

My Dear Boys: This is a complete story in itself, but forms the fourteenth volume of the "Rover Boys Series for Young Americans."

I started this series eleven years ago with the publication of the first three volumes, called "The Rover Boys at School," "On the Ocean" and "In the Jungle." I hoped the stories would be liked by the young folks, but I did not anticipate such a tremendously enthusiastic welcome as was accorded them. The publication of the third volume called for a fourth, "The Rover Boys Out West," and then followed "On the Great Lakes," "In the Mountains," "In Camp," "On Land and Sea," "On the River," "On the Plains," "In Southern Waters," "On the Farm" and then "On Treasure Isle."

For years the three brothers, Dick, Tom and Sam, had attended a military academy called Putnam Hall. But now their school days at that place were at an end, and in the present volume we find them going to college to finish their educations and fit themselves for their various stations in life. They are a bit older than they were, but just as wideawake and full of fun as ever, and just as determined to make records for themselves. They give a helping hand to some other students, help to win a famous football game, and thwart the efforts of some enemies who plot to get them into serious trouble. They also meet some of their old girl friends, the Lanings and Dora Stanhope, and—but perhaps I had better let that part of the story tell itself in the pages that follow.

Once again I thank my young friends for all the nice things they have said about these books, and I also thank the older folks who have said that they have read and enjoyed the stories. I trust the present volume will fulfil every reasonable expectation. And here's a handshake all around.

Affectionately and sincerely yours,

Edward Stratemeyer.

CONTENTS

THE ROVER BOYS AT

COLLEGE

CHAPTER I

ON THE TRAIN

"We're making time now, Tom."

"Making time?" repeated Tom Rover as he gazed out of the car window at the telegraph poles flashing past. "I should say we were, Sam! Why, we must be running sixty miles an hour!"

"If we are not we are making pretty close to it," came from a third boy of the party in the parlor car. "I think the engineer is trying to make up some of the time we lost at the last stop."

"That must be it, Dick," said Sam Rover. "Gracious, how we are rocking!" he added as the train rushed around a sharp curve and nearly threw him from his chair.

"I hope we get to Ashton on time," remarked Tom Rover. "I want to take a look around the college grounds before it gets dark."

"That's Tom, wanting to see it all before he sleeps!" cried Sam Rover with a grin. "You look out, Tom, that you don't get into disgrace the first thing, as you did when we went to Putnam Hall. Don't you remember that giant firecracker, and how Josiah Crabtree locked you up in a cell for setting it off?"

"Ugh! Will I ever forget it!" groaned Tom, making a wry face. "But I got the best of old Crabtree, didn't I?" he continued, his face brightening.

"Wonder if we'll make as many friends at col' lege as we did at Putnam Hall," remarked Dick Rover. "Those were jolly times and no mistake! Think of the feasts, and the hazings, and the baseball and football, and the rackets with the Pornell students, and all that!"

"Speaking of hazing, I heard that some of the hazing at the college we're bound for is fierce," came from Sam Rover.

"Well, we'll have to stand for what comes, Sam," answered his big brother. "No crying 'quit' here."

"Right you are, Dick," said Tom. "At the same time if—— Great Cæsar's ghost, what's up now!"

As Tom uttered the last words a shrill whistle from the locomotive pierced the air. Then came the sudden gripping of the air brakes on the car wheels, and the express came to a stop with a shock that pitched all the passengers from their seats. Tom and Sam went sprawling in a heap in the aisle and Dick came down on top of them.

"Hi, get off of me!" spluttered Sam, who was underneath.

"What's the matter? Have we run into another train?" asked Tom as he pushed Dick to one side and arose.

"I don't know," answered the older brother. "Something is wrong, that's certain."

"Are you hurt, Sam?" asked Tom as he helped the youngest Rover to his feet.

"No—not much," was the panting reply. "Say, we stopped in a hurry all right, didn't we?"

With the shock had come loud cries from the other people in the car, and it was found that one young lady had fainted. Everybody wanted to know what was the matter, but nobody could answer the question. The colored porter ran to the platform and opened the vestibule door. Torn followed the man and so did Sam and Dick.

"Freight train ahead, off the track," announced Tom. "We ran into the last car."

"Let us go up front and see how bad it is," returned Dick. "Maybe this will tie us up here for hours."

"Oh, I hope not," cried Sam. "I want to get to the college just as soon as possible. I'm dying to know what it's like."

"We can be thankful we were not hurt, Sam," said his older brother. "If our engineer hadn't stopped the train as he did we might have had a fearful smashup."

"I know it," answered Sam soberly, and then the boys walked forward to learn the full extent of the damage done and what prospects there were of continuing their journey.

To my old readers the lads just mentioned will need no special introduction, but for the benefit of those who have not read the previous volumes in this "Rover Boys Series" let me state that the brothers were three in number, Dick being the oldest, fun-loving Tom coming next and Sam the youngest. They were the sons of one Anderson Rover, a rich widower, and when at home lived with their father and an aunt and an uncle on a beautiful farm called Valley Brook.

From the farm, and while their father was in Africa, the boys had been sent by their Uncle Randolph to school, as related in the first book of the series, called "The Rover Boys at School." At this place, called Putnam Hall, they made many friends and also a few enemies and had "the time of their lives," as Tom often expressed it.

A term at school had been followed by a short trip on the ocean, and then the boys, in company with their uncle, went to the jungles of Africa to rescue Mr. Rover, who was a captive of a savage tribe of natives. After that came trips out West, and to the Great Lakes, and to the mountains, and, returning to school, the lads went into camp with the other cadets. Then they took another long trip on land and sea and led a Crusoe-like life on an island of the Pacific Ocean.

"I think we'd better settle down now," said Dick on returning home from being cast away, but this was not to be. They took a house-boat trip down the Ohio and the Mississippi rivers, had a number of adventures on the plains and then found themselves in southern waters, where they solved the mystery of a deserted steam yacht.

They returned to the farm and to Putnam Hall, and for a time matters went along quietly. On account of attending to some business for his father, Dick had fallen somewhat behind in his studies, and Tom and Sam did their best to catch up to him, and, as a consequence, all three of the youths graduated from Putnam Hall at the same time.

"And now for college!" Sam had said, and all were anxious to know where their parent intended to send them next. But instead of settling this question Mr. Rover came forward with a proposition that was as novel as it was inviting. This was nothing less than to visit a spot in the West Indies, known as Treasure Isle, and made a hunt for a large treasure secreted there during a rebellion in one of the Central American countries.

"A treasure hunt! Just the thing!" Dick had said, and his brothers agreed with him. The lads were filled with excitement over the prospect, and for the time being all thoughts of going to college were thrust aside.

From Mr. Rover it was learned that the treasure belonged to the estate of a Mr. Stanhope, who had died some years before. Mr. Stanhope's widow was well known to the Rover boys, and Dick thought that Dora Stanhope, the daughter, was the finest girl in the whole world. There was also another relative, a Mrs. Laning—the late Mr. Stanhope's sister—who was to share in the estate, and she had two daughters, Grace and Nellie, two young ladies who were especial favorites with Sam and Tom.

"Oh, we've got to find that treasure," said Tom, "Think of what it means to the Stanhopes and the Lanings."

"They'll be rich—and they deserve to be," answered his brother Sam. It may be added here that the Rovers were wealthy, so they did not begrudge the treasure to others.

A steam yacht was chartered and a party was made up, consisting of the Rovers, several of the boys' school chums, Mrs. Stanbope and Dora and, Mrs. Laning and Grace and Nellie. The steam yacht carried a fine crew and also an old tar called Bahama Bill, who knew the exact location of the treasure.

Before sailing it was learned that some rivals were also after the treasure. One of these was a sharper named Sid Merrick, who had on several occasions tried to get the best of the Rovers and failed. With Merrick was Tad Sobber, his nephew, a youth who at Putnam Hall had been a bitter foe to Dick, Tom and Sam. Sobber had sent the Rovers a box containing a live poisonous snake, but the snake got away and bit another pupil. This lad knew all about the sending of the reptile and he exposed Tad Sobber, and the latter, growing alarmed, ran away from the school.

The search for the treasure proved a long one, and Sid Merrick and Tad Sobber did all in their power to keep the wealth from falling into the haxids of the Rovers and their friends. But the Rovers won out in the quest and sailed away with tne treasure on board the steam yacht. The vessel of their enemies followed them, but a hurricane came up and the other ship was lost with nearly all on board.

"Well, that's the end of Sid Merrick and Tad Sobber," said Dick when he heard this news. "If they are at the bottom of the Atlantic Ocean they can't bother us any more." But Dick was mistaken in his surmise. It was true that Sid Merrick had been drowned, but Tad Sobber was alive, having been rescued by a schooner bound for London, and he was now on his way back to the United States, more bitter than ever against the Rovers, and with a determination to do all in his power to bring Dick, Tom and Sam to grief and gain possession of the money which he and his uncle had claimed belonged to them instead of to the Stanhope estate.

On arriving at Philadelphia from the West Indies the treasure was deposited in a strong box of a local trust company. From it the expenses of the trip were paid, and the sailors who had aided in the search were suitably rewarded. Later on the balance of the treasure was divided according to the terms of Mr. Stanhope's will. This placed a large sum of money in the hands of Mrs. Stanhope, both for herself and Dora, and also a goodly amount in the hands of Mrs. Laning for herself and Grace and Nellie.

The Stanhopes had always been fairly well off, but not so the Lanings. John Laning was a farmer, and this sudden change to riches bewildered him.

"Why, mother," he said to his wife, "whatever will you and the gals do with the money?"

"Several things, John," she answered. "In the first place, you are not going to work so hard and in the next place the girls are going to have a better education."

"Well, I'm not afraid of work," answered the farmer. "About eddication, if they want it— well, it's their money and they can have all the learnin' they want."

"Dora is going to a boarding school and Nellie and Grace want to go with her," went on Mrs. Laning.

"Where is Dora going?"

"To a place called Hope Seminary. Her mother knows the lady who is the principal."

"Well, if it's a good place, I reckon the gals can go too. But it will be terrible lonesome here without 'em."

"I know, John, but we want the girls to be somebody, now they have money, don't we?"

"Sure we do," answered Mr. Laning readily.

So it was arranged that the three girls should go to Hope Seminary, located several miles from the town of Ashton, in one of the Central States. In the meantime the Rover boys were speculating on what college they were to attend. Yale was mentioned, and Harvard and Princeton, and also several institutions located in the Middle West.

"Boys, wouldn't you like to go to Brill College?" asked their father one day. "That's a fine institution—not quite so large as some but just as good." And he smiled in a peculiar manner.

"Brill? Where is that?" asked Dick.

"It is near the town of Ashton, about two miles from Hope Seminary, the school Dora Stanhope and the Laning girls are going to attend." And Mr. Rover smiled again.

"Brill College for mine," said Sam promptly and in a manner that made his brothers laugh.

"Sam wants to be near Grace," said Tom.

"Well, don't you want to be near Nellie?" retorted the youngest Rover.

"Of course I do. And I reckon Dick won't be angry at being where he can occasionally see Dora," went on the fun-loving Rover with a sly wink. "Of course it's nice enough to write letters and send boxes of chocolates by mail, but it's a good deal better to take a stroll in the moonlight and hold hands, eh, Dick?"

"Is that what you do?" asked Dick, but his face grew very red as he spoke.

"Never in the wide, wide world!" cried Tom. "I leave that for my sentimental brothers, big and little."

"Who is sentimental?" exclaimed Sam. "Maybe I don't remember you and Nellie on the deck of the steam yacht that moonlight night——"

"Aw, cut it out!" muttered Tom. He turned to his father, who had been called from the room for a moment. "If you think Brill College a good one, dad, it will suit me."

"And it will suit me, too," added Sam.

"I mentioned Brill for two reasons," explained Mr. Rover. "The one was because it is near Hope Seminary and the other is because I happen to know the president, Dr. John Wellington, quite well; in fact, we went to school together. He is a fine gentleman—as fine a fellow as Captain Putnam—and I am sure his college must be a good one."

"If it's as good as dear old Putnam Hall, I shall be well content," answered Dick.

"Then you are satisfied to go there, Dick?"

"Yes, sir."

So it was settled and arrangements were at once made for the three boys to go to Brill. Fortunately it was found that their diplomas from Putnam Hall would admit them to the freshmen class without examination. All of the boys wrote letters to the girls and received answers in return. The college was to open two weeks before the seminary, so that to journey to Ashton together would be out of the question.

"Well, we'll see the girls later, anyway," said Dick. "I hope they like it at Hope and we like it at Brill; then we'll have some splendid times together."

"Right you are," answered Sam, and Tom said the same.

At last came the day for the boys to leave home. Trunks and dress-suit cases were packed, and not only their father but also their Uncle Randolph and their Aunt Martha went to the depot to see them off.

"Now be good and take care of yourselves," said Mr. Rover on parting.

"Learn all you can," added Uncle Randolph. "Remember that knowledge is better than wealth."

"Oh, I'm going to cram my head full of learning this trip," answered Tom with a grin.

"Take care of yourselves and don't get sick," was Aunt Martha's warning. "If you do, get a doctor right away." And then she gave each of the boys a warm, motherly kiss and a hug. She thought the lads the very best in all this wide world.

The train came and the boys were off. After a two hours' ride they had to change to the main line and got into the parlor car already mentioned. Then they had dinner in the diner and went back to the other car to read and to look at the scenery. Thus several hours slipped by, when of a sudden came the jar and shock that told them something out of the ordinary had happened.

CHAPTER II

AT THE SANDERSON HOUSE

When the Rover boys reached the head of the train they found an excited crowd beginning to collect. The locomotive of the express had cut into the last freight car a distance of several feet, smashing a number of boxes and barrels and likewise the headlight of the engine. Nobody had been hurt, for which everybody was thankful. But the engineer of the express was very angry.

"Why didn't you send a man back with a flag or put a torpedo on the track?" he demanded of the freight train conductor.

"Did send a man back," was the answer, "but he didn't go back far enough—hadn't time. This happened only a few minutes ago."

"You can't expect me to stop in a hundred feet," growled the engineer. As a matter of fact he had not stopped in many times that distance.

"Well, I did what I could," grumbled the freight conductor.

By making inquiries the Rover boys learned that the freight train had jumped a frog at a switch and part of the cars were on one track and part on another. Two trucks were broken, and nobody could tell how long it would take to clear the track upon which the express stood.

"May be an hour, but more likely it will be six or eight," said one of the brakemen to Tom. "This section of the road is the worst managed of the lot."

"And how far is it to Ashton?" asked Dick.

"About twelve miles by the railroad."

"Then walking is out of the question," came from Sam. "I shouldn't mind hoofing it if it was two or three."

"The railroad has to run around the hill yonder," went on the train hand. "If you go up the tracks for a quarter of a mile you'll come to a country road that will take you right into Ashton, and the distance from there isn't more than seven or eight miles."

"Any houses on that road?" asked Tom.

"Of course—farmhouses all along."

"Then come on," went on Tom to his brothers. "We can hire a carriage to take us to Ashton and to the college. Some farmer will be glad of the chance to earn the money."

"Let us wait and see if the train moves first," answered Dick.

"She won't move just yet," answered the brakeman with a sickly grin.

The boys stood around for a quarter of an hour and then decided to walk up to the country road that had been mentioned. Their trunks were checked through, but they had their dress-suit cases with them.

"We'll have to carry these," said Sam dolefully.

"Let us see if we can't check them," returned his big brother. But this was impossible, for the baggage car was locked and they could not find the man who had charge of it.

"Oh, well, come on," said Tom. "The cases are not so heavy, and it is a fine day for walking," and off he started and his brothers followed him.

It was certainly a fine day, as Tom said. It was early September, clear and cool, with a faint breeze blowing from the west. On the way they passed an apple orchard, laden with fruit, and they stopped long enough to get some.

"I declare this is better than sitting in that stuffy car," remarked Sam as he munched on an apple. "I am glad to stretch my legs."

"If we don't have to stretch them too long," remarked Dick.

"Say, I wonder if we'll pass anywhere near Hope Seminary!" cried Tom. "It may be on this road."

"What of it?" returned his younger brother. "The girls are not here yet—won't be for two weeks."

"Oh, we might get a view of the place anyway, Sam."

"I want to see Brill first," came from Dick. "If that doesn't suit us——" He ended with a sigh.

"Oh, it will suit, you can bet on it!" cried Sam. "Father wouldn't send us there if he wasn't sure it would be O. K. He's as much interested as we are."

Walking along the highway, which ran down to a little milk station on the railroad, the three boys soon discovered a farmhouse nestling between some trees and bushes. They threw their baggage on the grass and walked up to the front door.

They had to knock several times before their summons was answered. Then an old lady opened the door several inches and peeped out.

"What do you want?" she demanded in a cracked voice.

"Good afternoon," said Dick politely. "Can we hire somebody to drive us to Ashton? We were on the train, but there has been a smash-up, and we——"

"Land sakes alive! A smash-up, did you say?" cried the old lady.

"Yes, madam."

"Was my son Jimmie killed?"

"Nobody was killed or even hurt"

"Sure of that? My son Jimmie went to Crawford yesterday an' was coming back this afternoon. Sure he wasn't on that train?"

"If he was he wasn't hurt," answered Dick. "Can we hire a carriage to take us to Ashton?"

"How did it happen—that accident?"

"The express ran into the end of a freight train."

"Land sakes alive! The freight! Maybe it was the one we sent the cows away on. Was there any cows killed, do you know?"

"I don't think so."

"Well, tell me the particulars, will you? I don't go out much an' so I don't hear nuthin'. But an accident! Ain't it awful? But I always said it was risky to ride on the railroad; I told Jimmie so a hundred times. But he would go to Crawford an' now maybe he's a corpse. You are sure you didn't see a tall, thin young man, with a vrart on his chin, that was cut up?"

"What do you mean, the wart or the young man?" asked Tom, who was bound to have his fun.

"Why, the young man o' course; although I allow if he was cut up the wart would be, too. Poor boy! I warned him a hundred——"

"Can we hire a carriage here or not?" demanded Dick. The talk was growing a little tiresome to him.

"No, you can't!" snapped the old lady. "We never hire out our carriage. If we did it would soon go to pieces."

"Is there anybody who can drive us to Brill College? We'll pay for the service, of course."

"No. But you might get a carriage over to the Sanderson place."

"Where is that?" asked Sam.

"Up the road a piece," and the old lady motioned with her head as she spoke. "But now, if my son Jimmie was in that accident———"

"Good day, madam," said Dick and walked away, and Sam and Tom did the same. The old lady continued to call after them, but they paid no attention.

"Poor Jimmie! If he isn't killed in a railroad accident, he'll be talked to death some day," was Sam's comment.

"Don't you care. We know that Jimmie's got a wart, anyway," observed Tom, and he said this so dryly his brothers had to laugh. "Always add to your fund of knowledge when you can," he added, in imitation of his Uncle Randolph.

"I hope we have better success at the next farmhouse," said Sam. "I don't know that I want to walk all the way to Ashton with this dress-suit case."

"Oh, we're bound to find some kind of a rig at one place or another," said Dick. "All the folks can't be like that old woman."

They walked along the road until they came in sight of a second farmhouse, also set in among trees and bushes. A neat gravel path, lined with rose bushes, ran from the gate to the front piazza.

"This looks nice," observed Sam. "Some folks of the better sort must live here."

The three boys walked up to the front piazza and set down their baggage. On the door casing was an electric push button.

"No old-fashioned knocker here," observed Dick as he gave the button a push.

"Well, we are not wanting electric push buttons," said Tom. "An electric runabout or a good two-seat carriage will fill our bill."

The boys waited for fully a minute and then, as nobody came to answer their summons, Dick pushed the button again.

"I don't hear it," said Sam. "Perhaps it doesn't ring."

"Probably it rings in the back of the house," answered his big brother.

Again the boys waited, and while they did so all heard talking at a distance.

"Somebody in the kitchen, I guess," said Tom. "Maybe we had better go around there. Some country folks don't use their front doors excepting for funerals and when the minister comes."

Leaving their dress-suit cases on the piazza, the Rover boys walked around the side of the farmhouse in the direction of the kitchen. The building was a low and rambling one and they had to pass a sitting-room. Here they found a window wide open to let in the fresh air and sunshine.

"Now, you must go, really you must!" they heard in a girl's voice. "I haven't done a thing this afternoon, and what will papa say when he gets back?"

"Oh, that's all right, Minnie," was the answer in masculine tones. "You like us to be here, you know you do. And, remember, we haven't seen you in a long time."

"Yes, I know, Mr. Flockley, but———"

"Oh, don't call me Mr. Flockley. Call me Dudd."

"Yes, and please don't call me Mr. Koswell," broke in another masculine voice. "Jerry is good enough for me every time."

"But you must go now, you really must!" said the girl.

"We'll go if you'll say good-by in the right kind of a way, eh, Dudd?" said the person called Jerry Koswell.

"Yes, Minnie, but we won't go until you cib that," answered the young man named Dudd Flockley.

"Wha—what do you mean?" faltered the girl. And now, looking through the sitting-room window and through a doorway leading to the kitchen, the Rover boys saw a pretty damsel of sixteen standing by a pantry door, facing two dudish young men of eighteen or twenty. The young men wore checkered suits and sported heavy watch fobs and diamond rings and scarf-pins.

"Why, you'll give us each a nice kiss, won't you?" said Dudd Flockley with a smile that was meant to be alluring.

"Of course Minnie will give us a kiss," said Jerry Koswell. "Next Saturday I'm coming over to give you a carriage ride."

"I don't wish any carriage ride," answered the girl coldly. Her face had gone white at the mention of kisses.

"Well, let's have the kisses anyway!" cried Dudd Flockley, and stepping forward, he caught the girl by one hand, while Jerry Koswell grasped her by the other.

"Oh, please let me go!" cried the girl. "Please do! Oh, Mr. Flockley! Mr. Koswell, don't—don't—please!"

"Now be nice about it," growled Dudd Flockley.

"It won't hurt you a bit," added Jerry Koswell.

"I want you to let me go!" cried the girl.

"I will as soon as——" began Dudd Flockley., and then he gave a sudden roar of pain as he found himself caught by the ear. Then a hand caught him by the arm and he was whirled around and sent into a corner with a crash. At the same time Jerry Koswell was tackled and sent down in a heap in another corner. The girl, thus suddenly released, stared at the newcomers in astonishment and then sank down on a chair, too much overcome to move or speak.

CHAPTER III

LIKE KNIGHTS OF OLD

The Rover boys had acted on the impulse of the moment. They had seen that the girl wanted tSe two dudish young men to leave her alone, and stepping into the kitchen, Dick had tackled Dudd Flockley while Tom and Sam had given their attention to Jerry Koswell.

"You cowards!" cried Dick, confronting Flockley. "Why can't you leave a young lady alone when she tells you to?"

"They ought to be kicked out of the house," added Tom.

"You—you——" spluttered Dudd Flockley. He did not know what to say. He gathered himself up hastily and Jerry Koswell followed. "Who are you?" he demanded, facing Dick with clenched fists.

"Never mind who I am," was the reply of the oldest Rover. "Aren't you ashamed of yourself?"

"This is none of your affair," came from Koswell.

"Well, we made it our affair," answered Tom. He turned to the girl. "I hope we did right," he added hastily.

"Why—er—yes, I think so," faltered the girl. She was still very white and trembling. "But—but I hope you didn't hurt them."

"See here, Minnie, are you going to stand for this?" growled Dudd Flockley. "It ain't fair! We're old friends, and——"

"You had no right to touch me, Mr. Flockley," answered the girl. "I told you to let me go. I—I thought you were a—a—gentleman." And now the tears began to show in Minnie Sanderson's eyes.

"I am a gentleman."

"You didn't act like one."

"Oh, come, don't get prudish, Minnie," put in Jerry Koswell. "We didn't mean any harm. We——"

"I want you to leave this house!" said the girl, with a sudden show of spirit. "You had no warrant to act as you did. It—it was—was shameful! Leave at once!" And she stamped her small foot on the floor. Her anger was beginning to show itself and her face lost its whiteness and became crimson.

"We'll leave when we please," muttered Dudd Flockley.

"So we will," added Jerry Koswell.

On the instant Dick looked at his brothers, and the three advanced on the two dudish-lookingyoung men.

"You do as the young lady says," said Dick in a cold, hard voice. "I don't know you, but you are not wanted here, and that is enough. Go!" And he pointed to the door.

"See here——" blustered Flockley. But he got no further, for Dick suddenly wheeled him around and gave him a shove that sent him through the doorway and off the back porch.

"Now the other fellow," said the oldest Rover, but before Tom and Sam could touch Jerry Koswell that individual ducked and ran after Flockley. Then both young men stood at a safe distance.

"We'll fix you for this!" roared Flockley. "We don't know who you are, but we'll find out, and——"

"Maybe you want a thrashing right now," came from Tom impulsively. "I'm in fighting trim, if you want to know it." And he stepped out of the house, with Sam at his heels. Dick followed. At this hostile movement Flockley and Koswell turned and walked hurriedly out of the garden and down the country road, a row of trees soon hiding them from view.

"They are as mad as hornets," observed Sam. "If they belong anywhere near Ashton we'll have to look out for them."

"Right you are," answered Tom. "But I am not particularly afraid."

Having watched the two young men out of sign i, the three Rover boys returned to the farmhouse. Minnie Sanderson had now recovered somewhat and she blushed deeply as she faced them.

"Oh, wasn't it awful," she said. "I—I don't know what you think of it. They had no right to touch me. I thought they were gentlemen. They have called here several times, but they never acted that way before."

"Then we came in the nick of time," answered Dick. "Will you allow me to introduce myself?" and he bowed. "My name is Dick Rover and this is my brother Tom and this my brother Sam. You are Miss Sanderson, I suppose."

"Yes, Minnie Sanderson."

"We are strangers here. We were on the train, but there was a little accident and we were in a hurry to get to Ashton, so we got off and walked up this road, thinking we could hire somebody to drive us to Brill College."

"Oh, do you go to Brill?" And the girl's eyes opened widely.

"We don't go yet, but we are going."

"Then—then you'll meet Mr. Flockley and Mr. Koswell again."

"What, are they students there?" cried Tom.

"Yes. This is their second year, I believe. I know they were there last spring, for they called here."

Sam gave a low whistle.

"We are making friends first clip, aren't we?" he murmured to his brothers.

The boys related a few of the particulars of the accident and their experience at the farmhouse near the railroad.

"Oh, that's old Mrs. Craven!" cried Minnie Sanderson. "She would talk you out of your senses if you'd let her. But about a carriage, I don't know. If papa was here——"

At that moment came the sound of carriage wheels on the gravel path near the barn.

"There is papa now!" cried Minnie Sanderson. "You can talk to him. I guess he'll take you to the college quick enough."

"How did those two young fellows get here?" asked Sam.

"I don't know. And please—that is—you won't say anything to my father about that, will you? It would make him very angry, and I don't know what he'd do."

"We'll not say a word if you wish it that way," answered Dick.

"I don't think they'll bother me again after the way you treated them," added the girl.

She led them toward the barn and introduced her father, a fat and jolly farmer of perhaps fifty. Mr. Sanderson had been off on a short drive with one horse and he readily agreed to take them to Brill Cdlege for two dollars.

"Just wait till I put in a fresh team," he said. "Then I'll get you over to the college in less than an hour and a quarter."

While he was hooking up he explained that he had been to a nearby village for a dry battery for the electric doorbell.

"We don't use the bell much, but I hate to have it out of order," he explained.

"That's why it didn't ring," said Sam to his brothers.

The carriage was soon ready and the three dress-suit cases were piled in the rear. Then the boys got in and Mr. Sanderson followed.

"Good-by!" called the boys to Minnie Sanderson.

"Good-by," she returned sweetly and waved her hand.

"Maybe we'll get down this way again some day," said Dick.

"If you do, stop in," returned the girl.

The farmer's team was a good one and they trotted out of the yard and into the road in fine shape. Dick was beside the driver and his brothers were in the rear. The carriage left a cloud of dust behind as it bowled along over the dry country road.

"First year at Brill?" inquired Mr. Sanderson on the way.

"Yes," answered Dick.

"Fine place —no better in the world, so I've heard some folks say—and they had been to some of the big colleges, too."

"Yes, we've heard it was all right," said Tom. "By the way, where is Hope Seminary?"

"About two miles this side of Brill."

"Then we'll pass it, eh?" came from Sam.

"Well, not exactly. It's up a bit on a side road. But you can see the buildings—very nice, too—although not so big as those up to Brill. I'll point 'em out to you when we get there."

"Do you know any of the fellows at Brill?" questioned Tom, nudging Sam in the ribs as he spoke.

"A few. Minnie met some of 'em at the baseball and football games, and once in a while one of 'em stops at our house. But we are most too far away to see much of 'em."

Presently the carriage passed through a small village which the boys were told was called Rushville.

"I don't know why they call it that," said Mr. Sanderson with a chuckle. "Ain't no rushes growing around here, and there ain't no rush either; it's as dead as a salted mackerel," and he chuckled again. "But there's one thing here worth knowing about," he added suddenly.

"Whats' that?" asked Dick.

"The Jamison place—it's haunted."

"Haunted!" cried Tom. "What, a house?"

"Yes, a big, old-fashioned house, set in a lot of trees. It ain't been occupied for years, and the folks say it's haunted, and nobody goes near it."

"We'll have to inspect it some day," said Sam promptly.

"What—you?" cried the fat farmer.

"Sure."

"Ain't you scared?"

"No," answered the youngest Rover. "I don't believe in ghosts."

"Well, they say it's worth a man's life to go in that house, especially after dark."

"I think I'd risk it."

"So would I," added Tom.

"We'll pay the haunted house a visit some day when there is no session at the college," said Dick. "It will give us something to do."

"Hum!" mused the farmer. "Well, if you do it you've got backbone, that's all I've got to say. The folks around here won't go near that Jamison place nohow."

The road now became hilly, with many twists and turns, and the farmer had to give his entire attention to his team. The carriage bounced up and down and once Sam came close to being pitched out.

"Say, this is fierce!" he cried. "How much more of it?"

"Not more'n a quarter of a mile," answered Mr. Sanderson. "It is kinder rough, ain't it? The roadmaster ought to have it fixed. Some of the bumps is pretty bad."

There was one more small hill to cross, and then they came to a level stretch. Here the horses made good time and the farmer "let them out" in a fashion that pleased the boys very much.

"A fine team and no mistake," said Dick, and his pleased Mr. Sanderson very much, for he was proud of but two things—his daughter Minnie and his horses.

"There is Hope Seminary," said Mr. Sanderson presently and pointed to a group of buildings set in among some large trees. "That's a good school. I've been thinking of sending my daughter there, only it's a pretty long drive, and I need her at home. You see," he explained, "Minnie keeps house for me—has ever since my wife died, three years ago."

The boys gazed at the distant seminary buildings with interest, and as they did so Dick thought of Dora Stanhope and Tom and Sam remembered the Lanings. All thought how jolly it would be to live so close together during the college term.

"Now we've got only two miles more," said Mr. Sanderson as he set his team on a trot again. "I'll land you at Brill inside of fifteen minutes, even if the road ain't none of the best."

The country road ran directly into the town of Ashton, but there was a short cut to the college and they turned into this. Soon the lads caught sight of the pile of buildings in the distance. They were set in a sort of park, with the road running in front and a river in the rear. Out on the grounds and down by the stream the Rover boys saw a number of students walking around and standing in groups talking.

With a crack of his whip Mr. Sanderson whirled from the road into the grounds and drove up to the steps of the main building.

"This is the place where new students report," he said with a smile. "I'll take your grips over to the dormitory."

"Thank you, Mr. Sanderson," said Dick. "And here are your two dollars," and he handed the money over.

While Dick was paying the farmer Sam turned to the back of the carriage to look at the dress* suit cases. He gave an exclamation.

"What's the matter?" asked Tom.

"Didn't you have a suit case, Tom?"

"Certainly."

"Well, it's gone."

CHAPTER IV

WHAT HAPPENED AT THE CAMPUS FENCE

"Gone?"

"Yes, gone. Are you sure you put it in the carriage?"

"Positive," was Tom's answer. "I put it on top of yours and Dick's."

"Then it must have jounced out somewhere on the road."

"What's up?" asked Dick, catching a little of the talk.

"Tom's case is gone. He put it on top of ours, and I suppose coming over that rough road jounced it out."

"One of the satchels gone, eh?" came from Mr. Sanderson. "Sure you put it in?"

"Yes, I am positive."

"Too bad. Reckon I'd better go back at once and pick it up."

"I'll go with you," said Tom. The matter was talked over for a minute and then Tom and the farmer reëntered the carriage and drove off. As they did this a man came out to meet Dick and Sam.

"New students?" he asked shortly.

"Yes," replied Dick.

"Please step this way."

The doorman led them along a broad hall and into a large office. Here they signed a register and were then introduced by an under teacher to Dr. Wallington, a gray-haired man of sixty, tall and thin, with a scholarly aspect. The president of Brill shook hands cordially.

"I feel that I know you young gentlemen," he said. "Your father and I were old school chums. I hope you like it here and that your coming will do you much good."

"Thank you, I hope so too," answered Dick, and Sam said about the same. The two boys felt at once that the doctor would prove their friend so long as they conducted themselves properly, but they also felt that the aged president of Brill would stand for no nonsense.

Having been questioned by the doctor and one of the teachers, the boys were placed in charge of the house master, who said he would show them to their rooms in the dormitory. Dick had already explained the absence of Tom.

"Your father wrote that you would prefer to room together," said the house master. "But that will be impossible, since our rooms accommodate but two students each. We have assigned Samuel and Thomas to room No. 25 and Richard to room No. 26, next door."

"And who will I have with me?" asked Dick with interest. He did not much fancy having a stranger.

"Well, we were going to place a boy with you named Stanley Browne, a very fine lad, but day before yesterday we received a new application and the applicant said he desired very much to be put with the Rovers. So he can go with you, if you wish it."

"Who was the applicant?" asked Dick quickly.

"John A. Powell. He said he was an old school chum of yours at Putnam Hall and had been on a treasure hunt with you during the past summer."

"Songbird!" cried Dick, and his face broke out in a smile. "Oh, that's good news! It suits me perfectly."

"Did you call the young man Songbird?" queried the house master.

"Yes, that's his nickname."

"Then he must be a singer."

"No, he composes poetry—or at least verses that he calls poetry," answered the eldest Rover.

"I wish some more of the old Putnam Hall crowd were coming," put in Sam. "Think of having Hans Mueller here!" And the very idea made him grin.

"Hans isn't fit for college yet, Sam, But there may be others," added Dick hopefully.

They soon reached the dormitory, located across the campus from the main building and followed the house master up-stairs and to rooms No. 25 and 26. Each was bright, clean and cheerful, with big windows looking to the southward. Each contained two clothes closets, two beds, two bookshelves, a bureau, a reading table, two plain chairs and a rocker. The walls were bare, but the boys were told they could hang up what they pleased so long as they did not mar the plaster.

"The lavatories are at the end of the hall," said the house master. "And the trunk room is there, too. Have you had the trunks sent up yet?"

"No, sir," answered Dick.

"Then let me have your checks and I will attend to it. I see the man has already brought up your suit cases. I hope your brother has no trouble in recovering the one that was lost."

"When is John Powell coming?" asked Dick.

"To-morrow, so he telegraphed."

The house master left Dick and Sam and the two boys looked over the rooms and put some of the things from their suit cases in the closets and in the bureaus. Then they walked down to one of the lavatories and washed and brushed up. Everything was so new and strange to them that they did not feel at all at home.

"It will take a few days to get used to it I suppose," said Sam, with a trace of a sigh. "I know I felt the same way when first I went to Putnam Hall."

"Let us go down and take a look around and watch for Tom," replied his brother. "Say, but I'm glad Songbird is coming," he added. "I don't care much for his doggerel, but John's a good fellow just the same."

"None better," replied Sam heartily. "And his poetry isn't so very bad, always."

The two brothers went below and strolled around. They found the main building formed the letter T, with the top to the front. In this were the offices and the classroom and also the private apartments of the president and his family and some of the faculty. To the east of the main building was a long, one-story structure, containing a library and a laboratory, and to the west the three-story dormitory the lads had just left. Somewhat to the rear was another dormitory and beside it a large gymnasium, with a swimming pool attached. A short distance away was a house for the hired help and a stable and carriage sheds. Down by the river was a boathouse, not unlike that at Putnam Hall but larger.

"This is a fine layout and no mistake," observed Dick with satisfaction.

"Did you see that fine athletic field beyond the campus?" returned Sam. "That means baseball and football galore."

Having walked around the outside of the various buildings the Rover boys made their way to the highway to watch for the coming of Tom. Hardly had they reached the road when they saw a crowd of six students approaching. Among the number were Dudd Flockley and Jerry Koswell.

"See those two, Dick?" whispered Sam. "Won't they be mad when they see us here?"

"Well, I don't care," answered Dick coolly. "If they say anything, let me do the talking." And thus speaking, Dick sat down on the top of a stone fence and his brother hopped up beside him.

The six students came closer, and of a sudden Dudd Flockley espied the Rovers. He stopped short and pulled his crony by the arm, and Jerry Koswell likewise stared at Dick and Sam.

"You here?" demanded Flockley, coming closer and scowling at the youths on the fence.

"We are," answered Dick briefly.

"Freshmen?"

"Yes."

"Humph!" And Flockley put as much of a sneer as possible in the exclamation.

"How did you get here?" asked Koswell.

"Got a carriage at the Sanderson place," answered Sam with a grin.

"You did!" cried Flockley. "Say, you're a fresh lot, aren't you?" he went on, glaring at Dick and Sam. "Where's the third chap?"

"None of your business," answered Dick sharply.

"Don't you talk to me like that!" cried Dudd Flockley, and then his face took on a look of cunning. "Freshmen, eh? Then you don't know what we are. We are sophs, and we want you to answer us decently."

"That's the talk!" cried Koswell. "Boys, these are freshmen, and on the fence, too. We can't allow this, can we?"

"No freshies allowed on that fence!" answered another boy of the crowd. "Off you go and quick!"

As he spoke he approached Sam and tried to catch him by the foot to pull him off. Sam drew in his foot and then sent it forth so suddenly that it took the sophomore in the stomach and sent him reeling to the grass.

"At them!" yelled Flockley. "Show them how they must behave! Sophs to the front!"

"Wait!" The command came from Dick, and he spoke so clearly and firmly that all the sophomores paused. "Is this an affair between Flockley and Koswell and ourselves or is it simply two freshmen against six sophs?"

"Why—er—have Flockley and Koswell anything against you two?" demanded one of the boys curiously.

"I think so," answered Dick. "We had the pleasure of knocking them both down a few hours ago. As it was a private affair, we won't go into details."

"Didn't do it because you were freshmen?" asked another lad.

"Not at all. We were total strangers when the thing occurred."

"Yes, but——" came from another sophomore.

"Sorry I can't explain. Flockley and Koswell can if they wish. But I advise them to keep a certain party's name out of the story," added Dick significantly. He felt bound to protect Minnie Sanderson as much as possible.

"It's all stuff and nonsense!" roared Dudd Flockley. "They are freshies and ought to be bounced off the fence and given a lesson in the bargain."

"That's it—come and hammer 'em!" added Jerry Koswell.

"What's the row here?" demanded a tall lad who had just come up. He had light curly hair, blue eyes and a face that was sunshine itself.

"Two freshies on the stone fence, Holden," said one of the sophomores. "We can't allow that, you know."

At this Frank Holden, the leader of the sophomore class, laughed.

"Too bad, fellows, but they've got you. Term doesn't begin until to-morrow and they can sit where they please until twelve o'clock midnight. After that"—he turned to Dick and Sam—"well, your blood will be on your own heads if you disturb this fence or the benches around the flagstaff."

"My gracious! Frank's right, term isn't on until to-morrow," cried another student. "I beg your pardon, boys!" And he bowed lowly to the Rovers.

"Gee, it's a wonder you fellows wouldn't say something before I was kicked off the earth!" growled the sophomore who had been sent to the grass by Sam.

"Don't thank me for what I did," said Sam pleasantly, and this caused some of the other college fellows to grin.

"Don't say a word," cried the one who had gone down. "Only—well, if I catch you on the fence, it will be who's best man, that's all."

"Aren't we to do anything to these freshies?" demanded Dudd Flockley. He did not at all relish the turn affairs had taken.

"Can't do a thing until to-morrow," answered Frank Holden decidedly.

"Bah! I believe in making a freshie toe the mark as soon as he arrives."

"So do I," added Jerry Koswell.

"Can't be done—against the traditions of Brill," answered the class leader. "You've got to give a freshman time to get his feet planted on the ground, you know," he added kindly and with a smile at Dick and Sam.

"Thank you for that," answered the older Rover. "We'll be ready for the whole sophomore class by to-morrow."

"We'll see," answered Holden and passed on, and the majority of the second-year fellows followed. Flockley and Koswell lingered behind.

"See here, you chaps," said Flockley. "What are your names?"

"If you want to know so bad, my name is Dick Rover and this is my brother Sam."

"And who was the other fellow?" asked Koswell.

"My brother Tom."

"Three brothers, eh, and named Rover!" growled Dudd Flockley. "All right, I'll remember that, and I'll remember how you treated us up to the Sanderson place."

"And I'll remember it too and square up," added Koswell.

"We'll make Brill too hot to hold you," snapped Flockley, and then he turned into the gateway leading to the campus and his crony followed.

CHAPTER V

GETTING ACQUAINTED

"Dick, we have made two enemies, that's sure," remarked Sam to his brother as they watched Flockley and Koswell depart.

"It couldn't be helped if we have, Sam," was the reply. "You are not sorry for what we did at the Sanderson house, are you?"

"Not in the least. What we should have done was to give those chaps a sound thrashing."

"They seem to have a number of friends here. Probably they will do all they can to make life at this college miserable for us."

"Well, if they do too much, I reckon we can do something too."

Some new students had been standing at a distance watching the scene described in the last chapter. Now one of them approached and nodded pleasantly.

"Freshmen?" he asked.

"Yes," answered both of the Rovers.

"So am I. My name is Stanley Browne. What's yours?"

"Dick Rover, and this is my brother Sam."

"Oh, are you Dick Rover? I've heard about you. My cousin knows you real well."

"Who is your cousin?"

"Larry Colby."

"Larry!" cried Dick. "Well, I guess he does know us well. We've had some great times together at Putnam Hall and elsewhere. So you are Larry's cousin? I am real glad to know you."

And Dick held out his hand.

"Larry is one of our best chums," said Sam, also shaking hands. "I remember now that he has spoken of you. I am glad to know somebody at this place." And Sam smiled broadly. Soon all three of the boys were on good terms, and Stanley Browne told the Rovers something about himself.

"I come from the South," he said. "My folks own a large cotton plantation there. Larry was down there once and we had a lot of fun. He told me of the sport he had had with you. You must have had great times at Putnam Hall."

"We did," said Sam.

"I thought there were three of you, from what Larry said."

"So there are," answered Dick, and told about Tom and the missing dress-suit case. "Tom ought to be getting back," he added.

Stanley had been at Brill for two days and had met both Flockley and Koswell. He did not fancy either of the sophomores.

"That Frank Holden is all right," he said, "but Flockley and Koswell are very overbearing and dictatorial. I caught them ordering one of the freshmen around like a servant. If they had spoken that way to me I'd have knocked them down." And the eyes of the Southern lad flashed darkly.

"Where do you room?" asked Dick. He remembered what the house master had said about Stanley and felt that the youth would make a nice roommate for anybody.

"I'm in No. 27, right next to you fellows. Mr. Hicks was going to put me in with you first, but afterward said a friend of yours was going to fill the place."

"Yes," said Dick. "But you will be right next door, so it will be almost the same thing. Who is your roommate?"

"A fellow named Max Spangler. I don't know much about him, as he only came this noon. But he seems all right. Here he comes now."

As Stanley spoke he motioned to a short, stout lad who was walking across the campus. The boy had a distinctly German face and one full of smiles.

"Hello, Friend Browne," he called out pleasantly and with a German accent. "Did you find somebody you know?"

"I've made myself known," answered Stanley,, and then he introduced the others. "They bunk next door to us," he added with a nod toward Dick and Sam.

"Hope you don't snore," said Max Spangler. "I can go anybody but what snores."

"No, we don't snore," answered Sam, laughing.

"Then I'm your friend for life and two days afterward," answered the German-American lad, and said this so gravely the others had to laugh. Max put the Rovers in mind of their old friend Hans Mueller, but he spoke much better English than did Hans, getting his words twisted only when he was excited.

Dick suggested that they all walk down the road to meet Tom, and this was done. The conversation was a lively one, Stanley and Max telling of their former schooldays and the Rovers relating a few of their own adventures. Thus the four got to be quite friendly by the time the carriage with Tom and Mr. Sanderson came in sight.

"Find it?" sang out Sam to his brother.

"No," was Tom's reply.

"You didn't!" cried Dick. "How far back did you go?"

"Way back to Rushville. I know it was in the carriage at that place, for I saw it."

"Too bad," said Sam. "Did you have much of value in it?"

"Not a great deal. Most of my stuff is in my trunk. But the case alone was worth six dollars, and it had my comb and brush and toothbrush and all those things in it."

"Want me any more?" asked Mr. Sanderson. "If you don't, I'll get home. It's past milking time now."

"No, I'll not need you," answered Tom and hopped to the ground. A minute later the farmer turned his team around and was gone in a cloud of dust.

Tom was introduced to Stanley and Max, and the whole crowd walked slowly back to the college grounds. Then Tom was taken to his room, the others going up-stairs with him. He washed and brushed up, went to the office and registered, and then the bell rang for supper.

The dining hall at Brill was a more elaborate affair than the messroom at Putnam Hall, but the Rovers were used to dining out in fine places, so they felt perfectly at home. Dick and Sam had already met the instructor who had charge of their table, Mr. Timothy Blackie, and they introduced Tom. Stanley and Max were at the same table and also a long-haired youth named Will Jackson, although his friends called him "Spud."

"I don't know why they call me Spud," he said to Dick, "excepting because I like potatoes so, I'd rather eat them than any other vegetable. Why, when I was out in Jersey one summer, on a farm, I ate potatoes morning, noon and night and sometimes between times. The farmer said I had better look out or I'd sprout. I guess I ate about 'steen bushels in three weeks."

"Phew!" whistled Sam. "That's a good one."

"Oh, it's a fact," went on Spud. "Why, one night I got up in my sleep and they found me down in the potato bin, filling my coat pockets with potatoes, and——"

"Filling your coat pocket?" queried Stanley.

"Do you sleep with your coat on?"

"Why, I—er—I guess I did that night," answered Will Jackson in some confusion. "Anyway, I'm a great potato eater," he added lightly. Later on the others found out that Spud had a vivid imagination and did not hesitate to "draw the long bow" for the sake of telling a good story.

The meal was rather a stiff and quiet one among the new students, but the old scholars made the room hum with talk about what had happened at the previous term. There was a good bit of conversation concerning the last season of baseball and more about the coming work on the gridiron. From the talk the Rovers gathered that Brill belonged to something of a league composed of several colleges situated in that territory, and that they had held the football championship four and three seasons before, but had lost it to one of the colleges the next season and to another college the season just past.

"Football hits me," said Dick to Stanley. "I'd like to play first-rate."

"Maybe you'll get a chance on the eleven, although I suppose they give the older students the preference," was the reply.

Stanley had met quite a few of the other students, and after supper he introduced the Rovers and Max and also Spud. Thus the Rovers were speedily put on friendly terms with a score or more of the freshmen and also several of the others. One of the seniors, a refined young man named Allan Charter, took the crowd through the library and the laboratory and also down to the gymnasium and the boathouse.

"We haven't any boat races, for we have no other college to race against," said the senior. "The students sometimes get up contests between themselves, though. Dick Dawson used to be our best oarsman, but last June a fellow named Jerry Koswell beat him."

"Koswell!" cried Sam. "I thought he was too much of a dude to row in a race."

At this remark the senior smiled faintly.

"Evidently you have met Mr. Koswell," he remarked pointedly.

"We have," answered Tom.

"Well, he can row, if he can't do anything else."

"I'd like to try my skill against him some day," said Tom, who during the past year had taken quite a fancy to rowing.

"Perhaps Koswell will be glad to let you have the chance," said Allan Charter.

A little later the senior left the freshmen, and the latter strolled back in the direction of the college buildings. It was now growing dark, and the Rovers concluded to go up to their rooms and unpack their trunks, which had just come in from the depot.

"You fellows want to keep your eyes wide open to-night," cautioned Stanley, who came up with them.

"Hazing?" asked Dick.

"So I was told."

"Will they start in so early?" asked Sam.

"Any time after midnight. I hate to think of it, but I reckon a fellow has got to submit."

"That depends," answered Dick. "I'll not stand for everything. I'll not mind a little hazing, but it mustn't be carried too far."

"That's the talk," cried Tom. "If they go too far—well, we'll try to give 'em as good as they send, that's all."

"Right you are!" came from Sam.

They unpacked their trunks and proceeded to make themselves at home as much as possible. As Dick was alone in his room, he went over to his brothers' apartment for company, locking his door as he did so.

"I'll tell you what I'd do if I were you, Dick," said Tom. "Stay here to-night. My bed is big enough for two on a pinch. Then, if there is any hazing, we can keep together. To-morrow, if Songbird comes, it will be different."

This suited the oldest Rover, and he brought over such things as he needed for the night. The boys were tired out, having put in a busy day, and by ten o'clock Sam and Tom were both yawning.

"I think I'll go to bed," said Sam. "If anything happens wake me up."

"Oh, you'll wake up fast enough if they come," answered Tom. "But I am going to lay down myself. But I am not going to undress yet."

Taking off their shoes and collars, ties and coats, the boys said their prayers and laid down. Sam was soon in the land of dreams, and presently Tom and Dick followed.

Two hours passed and the three lads were sleeping soundly, when suddenly Tom awoke with a yell. A stream of cold water had struck him in the head, making him imagine for the instant that he was being drowned.

"Hi, stop!" he spluttered and then stopped, for the stream of water took him directly in the mouth. Then the stream was shifted and struck first Dick and then Sam. All three of the Rovers leaped from the beds as quickly as possible. Although confused from being awakened so rudely, they realized what it meant.

They were being hazed.

CHAPTER VI

A HAZING, AND WHAT FOLLOWED

The stream of water came from a small hose that was being played through a transom window over the door of the room. A lad was holding the hose, and in the dim light Dick recognized the face of a youth named Bart Larkspur, a sophomore who did not bear a very good reputation. Larkspur was poor and Dick had heard that he was used by Flockley, Koswell and others to do all sorts of odd jobs, for which the richer lads paid him well.

"Stop that, you!" cried the oldest Rover, and then, rushing to the door, he flung it open and gave a shove to what was beyond. This was a short step-ladder upon which Larkspur and several others were standing, and over the ladder went with a crash, sending the hazers to the floor of the hallway in a heap.

"Get the hose," whispered Tom, who had followed his brother, and while the sophomores were endeavoring to get up, he caught the squirming hose and wrenched it, nozzle and all, from Bart Larkspur's hand.

"Hi, give me that!" yelled Larkspur.

"All right, here you are," answered Tom merrily, and turned the stream of water directly in the sophomore's face. Larkspur spluttered and shied and then plunged to one side into a fellow student standing near. This was Dudd Flockley, and he was carried down on his back.

"Play away, Six!" called out Tom in true fireman style, and directed the stream on Flockley. It hit the dudish student in the chin and ran down inside his shirt collar.

"Stop, I beg of you! Oh, my!" screamed Flockley, trying to dodge the water. "Larkspur, grab the hose! Knock that rascal down! Why don't somebody do something?"

"Give me that hose, you freshie!" called out Jerry Koswell, who was in the crowd. "Don't you know better than to resist your superiors? I want you to understand——"

"Keep cool, old man, don't get excited," answered Tom brazenly. "Ah, I see you are too warm. Will that serve to keep your temperature down?" And now he turned the hose on Koswell, hitting the fellow directly in the left ear. Koswell let out a wild yell and started to retreat and so did several others.

"Don't go! Capture the hose!" called out Flockley, but even as he spoke he took good care to get behind another sophomore.

"Capture it yourself!" growled the youth he was using as a shield.

"Say, you're making too much noise," whispered another student. "Do you want the proctor down on us? And turn that water off before you ruin the building. Somebody has got to pay for this, remember," he added.

As it was an unwritten law of Brill that all hazers must pay for any damage done to college property while hazing anybody, one of the sophomores started for the lavatory where the hose had been attached to a water faucet. But while the water still ran, Tom, aided by Dick and Sam, directed the stream on the sophomores, who were forced to retreat down the hallway.

"Now rush 'em! Rush 'em!" yelled Flockley, when the water had ceased to run. "Bind and gag 'em, and take 'em down to the gym. We can finish hazing 'em there!"

"Get into the room!" whispered Dick. "Hurry up, and barricade the door!"

"Right you are, but no more hose water for me," answered Tom, and pulled on the rubber

THE STREAM OF WATER TOOK HIM DIRECTLY IN THE MOUTH.—*Page* 55.

The Rover Boys at College.

with all his might. It parted about half way down the hallway, and into the room he darted with the piece in his hands. Then Sam and Dick closed the door, locked it, and shoved a bed and the table against the barrier. They also turned the button of the transom window so that the glass could not be swung back as before.

"Now they can't get in unless they break in," said Dick grimly, "and I doubt if they'll dare to do that."

"Say, maybe I'm not wet," remarked Sam, surveying his dripping shirt.

"Never mind; we sent as good as we got, and more," answered Tom with a grin. "Let us put on our coats so we don't catch cold. No use of putting on dry clothing until you are sure the ball is over."

"Tom, you're a crack fireman," said Dick with a smile. "I'll wager those sophs are mad enough to chew nails."

"What's sauce for the goose is sauce for the gander," quoted the fun-loving Rover. "What's the good of living if you can't return a compliment now and then?"

For several minutes all was silent outside. Then came a light knock on the door. Dick held his hand up for silence and the knock was repeated.

"Don't answer them," whispered the oldest Rover.

"Say, I want to talk to you fellows," came in low tones. "This is important."

Who are you?" asked Dick after a pause.

"I'm Larkspur—Bart Larkspur. I want to tell you something."

"Well; what is it?" demanded Tom.

"Your resistance to our class won't do you any good. If you'll come out and take your medicine like men, all right; but if you resist it will go that much harder with you."

"Who sent you—Frank Holden?" asked Sam.

"What has Holden to do with it?" growled Larkspur.

"We know he's the leader of your class."

"He is not. Dudd Flockley is our leader."

"Then Flockley sent you, eh?" put in Dick.

"Yes, if you want to know it."

"Well, tell Flockley to mind his own business," answered Dick sharply. "If Frank Holden wants us we'll come, but not otherwise."

"Are you hazing any of the other fellows?" asked Tom.

"We'll haze them after we get through with you," growled Larkspur, and then the Rovers heard him tiptoe his way down the hall.

"I think this attack was gotten up by the Flockley-Koswell crowd," was Dick's comment. "Maybe it wasn't sanctioned by the other sophs at all."

The Rovers waited a while longer and then with caution they pulled back the bed and the table and opened the door. By the dim light in the hallway they saw that the place was deserted. Somebody had run a mop over the polished floor, thus taking up most of the water.

"I guess they have given it up for to-night," said Dick, and his words proved correct.

After waiting a good hour the three Rovers rearranged the room, hanging up some of the bedding and rugs to dry near the window, which they left wide open. Then they locked the door and went into Dick's room, which had not been disturbed. As they did this another door opened, and Stanley poked out his head, followed by Max.

"We heard it all," said the Southern lad with a chuckle. "Hope you doused 'em good!"

"We did," answered Tom. "They didn't tackle you, did they?"

"No; but I suppose they will later, or to-morrow."

"I am ready for them if they come," came from Max. "I got this," and he held up a long, white sack.

"What is it?" asked Sam.

"Plaster of Paris. If they tackle me I'll make 'em look like marble statues already." And the German-American youth winked one eye suggestively.

Despite the excitement the Rover boys slept soundly for the rest of the night. All were rather sleepy in the morning, but a good wash in cold water brightened them greatly. While getting ready for breakfast they looked for Flockley and Koswell, but those two students, as well as Larkspur, kept out of sight.

"They don't like the way matters turned out last night," said Dick.

On entering the dining-room they saw the sophomores at a nearby table. Flockley and Koswell glared darkly, while as they passed, Larkspur put out his foot to trip Sam up. But Sam was on guard, and instead of stumbling he stepped on the fellow's ankle, something that caused Larkspur to utter a gasp of pain.

"What did you do that for?" he demanded savagely.

"Sorry, but you shouldn't sprawl all over with your feet," answered the youngest Rover coldly, and passed on to his seat. When he looked back, Larkspur, watching his chance so that no teacher might see him, shook his fist at Sam.

"We have got to keep our eyes wide open for that bunch," was Dick's comment. "Last night's affair will make Flockley and Koswell more sour than ever, and Larkspur is evidently their tool, and willing to do anything they wish done."

After chapel the Rovers were assigned to their various classes and given their text-books. It was announced that no regular classes would be called until the following Monday morning.

"That gives us plenty of time to study our first lessons," said Sam.

"Yes, and gives us time to get acquainted with the college layout and the rest of the students," added Tom. "Do you know, I think I am going to like it bang-up here."

"Just what I was thinking," returned Dick. "It isn't quke so boyish as Putnam Hall was— some of the seniors are young men—but that doesn't matter. We are growing older ourselves."

"Gracious, I'm not old!" cried Tom. "Why, I feel like a two-year-old colt!" And to prove his words he did several steps of a jig.

Only about half of the students had as yet arrived, the others being expected that day, Friday, and Saturday. The college coach was to bring in some of the boys about eleven o'clock, and the Rovers wondered if Songbird Powell would be among them.

"You'll like Songbird," said Dick to Stanley Browne. "He's a great chap for manufacturing what he calls poetry, but he isn't one of the dreamy kind—he's as bright and chipper as you find 'em."

The boys walked down to the gymnasium, and there Sam and Tom took a few turns on the bars and tried the wooden horses. While they did this Dick talked to a number of the freshmen with whom he had become acquainted.

"We are to have a necktie rush Monday," said one boy. "Every fellow is to wear the college colors. Meet on the campus an hour before supper time."

"I'll be there," said Dick. He knew what was meant by a necktie rush. All the freshmen would don neckties showing the college colors, and the sophomores, and perhaps the juniors, would do their best to get the neckties away from them. If more than half the boys lost their ties before the supper bell rang the freshmen would be debarred from wearing the colors for that term.

Shortly before eleven o'clock a shout was heard on the road, and a number of the students made a rush in that direction. The college coach swung into sight in a cloud of dust. It was fairly overflowing with boys and young men, all yelling and singing and waving their hats and caps. At the sight those on the campus set up a cheer.

"This is something like!" cried Tom enthusiastically. He wanted to see things "warm up," as he expressed it.

The coach was followed by three carriages, and all deposited their loads at the main building steps and on the campus. There were more cheers and many handshakes.

"There he is!" cried Sam, and rushing forward, he caught John Powell by the hand, shook it, and relieved the newcomer of his suit case.

"Hello, Sam!" cried Songbird, and grinned from ear to ear. "Hello, Dick! Hello, Tom! Say, did I surprise you?" And now he shook hands with the others.

"You sure did," repl&d Dick. "I was afraid I was going to have a stranger for a roommate. Your coming here suits me to a T!"

"I didn't write to you because I wanted to surprise you," explained Songbird. "I've composed some verses about it. They start——"

"Never mind the verses now," interrupted Tom. "Come on in and we'll introduce you to the fellows, and then we'll listen to your story. And we'll tell you some things that will surprise you."

"And I'll tell you some things that will surprise you, too," returned John Powell, as he was led away by the three Rover boys.

CHAPTER VII

THE ARRIVAL OF SONGBIRD

"So you've made some enemies as well as some friends, eh?" remarked Songbird Powell, after he had been registered, taken up to his room, and had listened to what the Rover boys had to tell. "No use of talking, it doesn't take you fellows long to stir things up!"

"You said you had a surprise for us, Songbird," returned Tom. "I'm dying by inches to know what it is."

"Maybe it's a new poem," put in Sam with a grimace at his brothers.

"I've got a poem—several of them, in fact," answered Songbird, "but I didn't have those in mind when I spoke. Who do you suppose I met yesterday morning, in Ithaca, while I was waiting for the train?"

"Dora Stanhope and the Lanings," answered Tom promptly.

"No. Tad Sobber."

"Tad Sobber!" exclaimed the Rover boys in concert.

"Songbird, are you sure of it?" demanded Dick.

"Sure? Wasn't I talking to him!"

"But—but—I thought he was lost in that hurricane, when the *Josephine* was wrecked."

"No. It seems he escaped to a vessel bound for England; but his uncle, Sid Merrick, was lost, and so were most of the others. Sobber just got back from England came in on one of the ocean liners, so he told me."

"How did he act?" asked Tom.

"Where was he going?" added Sam.

"Did he seem to have any money?" came from Dick.

All of the Rovers were intensely interested, and showed it plainly.

"Say, one question at a time, please!" cried Songbird. "You put me in mind of a song I once wrote about a little boy:

"'A little lad named Johnny Spark
Was nothing but a question mark.
He asked his questions night and day,
When he was resting or at play.
One minute he would tackle pa,
And then he'd turn and tackle ma;
And then his uncle he would quiz——'"

"And let that line please end the biz,"

finished Tom. "Say, Songbird, please don't quote poetry when we are waiting to hear all about Tad Sobber. Have some pity on us."

"Yes, tell us of Sobber," added Sam and Dick.

"All right, if you don't appreciate my verses," returned the would-be poet with a sigh.

"Well, to start with, Tad Sobber was well dressed, and looked as if he had all the money he needed. He wore a brown checkered suit, so evidently he hasn't gone into mourning for his uncle. He told me he had had a rough experience on the ocean during the hurricane, and he blames you Rovers for all his troubles."

"That's just like Sobber," was Dick's comment.

"He wouldn't tell me where he was going or what he was going to do, but he did let drop a remark or two about the fortune you discovered on Treasure Isle. He said that he was firmly convinced that the money belonged to him and to his uncle's estate, and that he meant some day to make a fight for it."

"In the courts?" asked Tom. "If he does that he'll get beaten. Father says the treasure belongs to the Stanhope estate and to nobody else."

"No, he didn't say he was going to court about it, but he said he was bound to get hold of it some day."

"I hope he doesn't try to get it by force," said Sam. "That would mean trouble for the Stanhopes and the Lanings."

"The money is in the banks now, Sam," said Dick. "He couldn't get hold of it excepting on an order from those to wtiom it belongs."

"And they'll never give him any such order," added Tom.

"Do you suppose he was going to see the Stanhopes and the Lanings?" questioned the oldest Rover anxiously.

"He didn't say. I wanted to question him further, but a man who was standing on a corner, some distance away, beckoned to him, and he left me and joined the man, and the two walked off."

"Who was the man?"

"I don't know."

The boys talked the matter over for some time, but Songbird had nothing more to tell, and at last the subject was dropped. Songbird was introduced to Stanley, Max, and a number of the other students, and soon he felt quite at home.

That evening there was a bit of hazing. Dick and Tom escaped, but Sam, Songbird and Stanley were caught in the lower hallway by a number of the sophomores and carried bodily to the gymnasium, Here they were tossed in blankets and then blindfolded.

"We'll take them to the river," said one of the sophomores. "A bath will do them good."

"Let's give 'em a rubbing down with mud!" cried Jerry Koswell. He had some tar handy, and if the mud was used he intended to mix some of the tar with it on the sly.

"That's the talk!" cried Larkspur, who knew about the tar, he having purchased it for Koswell and Flockley. The three had at first intended to smear the beds of the Rovers with it, but had gotten no chance.

"Give them a good dose!" said Dudd Flockley. He had joined in the blanket-tossing with vigor.

Sam, Songbird and Stanley were being led to the river when Max came rushing up to Tom and Dick, who happened to be in the library, looking over some works of travel.

"Come on mit you!" he cried excitedly in broken English. "Da have got Sam and Stanley and dot friend of yours alretty! Hurry up, or da was killed before we git to help 'em!"

"They? Who?" asked Dick, leaping up.

"Sophs—down by der gym!" And then Max cooled down a bit and related what he had seen.

"We must surely go to the rescue!" cried Tom. "Wait! I'll get clubs for all hands!" And he rushed up to his room, where in a clothing closet lay the end of the hose he had taken away from the sophomores. With his knife he cut the section of hose into eight "clubs," and with these in his hands he hurried below again.

At a cry from Dick and Max the freshmen commenced to gather on the campus, and Tom quickly handed around the sections of hose. Other first-year lads procured sticks, boxing gloves, and other things, and looked around for somebody to lead them.

"Come on!" cried Dick, and he sprang to the front, with Tom on one side and Max on the other. The German-American boy had a big squirtgun filled with water, a gun used by the gardener for spraying the bushes.

The sophomores had captured four more freshmen, and marched all of the crowd down to the river front, when the band under Dick, sixteen strong, appeared. The latter came on yelling like Indians, and flourishing their sections of hose, and sticks and other things.

"Let 'em go! Let 'em go!" was the rallying cry, and then whack! whack! whack! down came the rubber clubs and the sticks on the backs of the second-year students.

"Fight 'em off!" came from the sophomores.

"Chase 'em away!" yelled Dudd Flockley; but hardly had he spoken when Max discharged the squirtgun, and the water took Flockley in the eye, causing him to yell with fright and retreat. Then Max turned the gun on Larkspur, soaking the latter pretty thoroughly.

Attacked from the rear, the sophomores had to let go their holds on their victims, and as soon as they were released Sam, Songbird and the others ran to the right and the left and joined the force under Dick.

All told, the freshmen now numbered twenty-three, while the sophomores could count up but fourteen. The second-year students were hemmed in and gradually forced nearer and nearer to the bank of the river.

"Let up! let up!" yelled several in alarm. "Don't knock us overboard!"

"It's nothing but mud here! I don't want my new suit spoiled!" cried one.

"I can't swim!" added another.

"I've got an idea," whispered Tom to the others near him. "Shove 'em in the mud and water, or else make 'em promise not to take part in the necktie rush."

"That's the talk!" replied Dick. He caught hold of the sophomore in front of him. "All shove, fellows!" And the second-year students were gradually forced to the very edge of the river at a point where there was a little water and a good deal of dark, sticky mud. Of course they fought desperately to push the freshmen back, but they were outnumbered, as already told.

"Now, then, every fellow who will promise not to take part in the necktie rush Monday will be allowed to go free," said Dick loudly. "The others must take their ducking in the water— and mud."

"Let me go!" roared Dudd Flockley. "I'm not going to have this suit ruined!"

"I don't want to get these patent leathers wet!" cried Jerry Koswell, who had on a new pair of shiny shoes.

"Then promise!" cried Sam, and "Promise!" "Promise!" came from many others.

Without delay several of the sophomores promised, and they were allowed to depart. Then the others began to show fight, and three managed to escape, among them being Dudd Flockley. The others were forced into the water and mud up to their knees. Then they cried out in alarm, and while two finally escaped, the others also promised to keep out of the necktie contest.

"Just wait!" snarled Jerry Koswell as he at last managed to pull himself out of the sticky mud. "Just wait, that's all!" His patent-leather shoes were a sight to behold.

"Not so much fun when you are hazed yourself, is it?" asked Sam coolly.

"We'll give it to 'em yet," put in Bart Larkspur. "Lots of time between now and the closing of the term." And then he and Koswell ran off to join Dudd Flockley. The three went to their rooms and cleaned up as best they could, and then took a walk down the road in the direction of Rushville.

"It was that Dick Rover who led the attack," said Dudd Flockley. "Do you know what I think? I think he is going to try to make himself leader of the freshies."

"Just what I thought, too," answered Larkspur. "And if that's the fact we ought to do all we can to pull him down."

"Tom Rover is the fellow I am going to get after," came from Jerry Koswell. He had not forgotten how Tom and Sam had sent him to the floor in the presence of Minnie Sanderson.

The three students walked a distance of half a mile when they saw approaching them a trampish-looking man carrying what looked to be a new dress-suit case. They looked at the fellow rather sharply and he halted as he came up to them.

"Excuse me," he mumbled, "but did any of you gents lose this case?"

"Why, it must be Rover's case!" cried Flockley. Nearly every one in the college had heard about the missing baggage.

"I found it in the bushes alongside the road," went on the tramp. "Thought it might belong to some of the college gents."

"Let me look at it," said Koswell, and turned the case around. "Yes, it's Rover's," he added, seeing the initials and the address.

"Better take it up to the college," put in Larkspur.

"Wait, I'll take it up," said Jerry Koswell suddenly. "This belongs to a poor chap," he added to the tramp. "He won't be able to reward you, but I will. Here's a quarter for you." And he passed over the silver piece.

"Much obliged," said the tramp. "Want me to carry it up to the buildings?"

"No, I'll do that," said Koswell, and then he winked at his cronies. The tramp went on and the three watched him disappear in the distance.

"What did you do that for, Jerry?" asked Flockley with interest. He surmised that something new was afoot.

"Oh, I did it for the fun of the thing," answered Koswell coolly. "But maybe I can work it in somehow against that Rover bunch. Anyway, I'll try."

CHAPTER VIII

THE COLORS CONTEST

The next morning Tom was much surprised to find his missing dress-suit case standing in front of his room door.

"Hello! How did this get here?" he cried as he picked up the baggage.

"What's that?" asked Sam, who was just getting up.

"Look!" answered his brother, and brought the case in. "Somebody must have found it and left it here while I was asleep."

"Very kind, whoever he was," said Sam. "Are the contents all right?"

Instead of answering Tom placed the suit case on a chair and started to unlock it.

"Hello, it's unlocked!' he murmured. "I thought I had it locked."

He shoved back the clasps and threw the case open. The contents were much jumbled, but he had expected this from the fact that the bag had been jounced out of the carriage.

"I guess the stuff is all here," he said slowly, turning over the clothing and other things. "Somehow, I thought I had more in the case, though," he added presently.

"Don't you know what you had?"

"Well—er—I packed it in a hurry, you know. I wanted to go fishing, and so I got through as soon as I could. Oh, I guess it's all right."

Tom was too lively a youth to pay much attention to his personal belongings. Often he hardly knew what suit of clothing he had on or what sort of a necktie. The only times he really fixed up was when Nellie Laning was near. Why he did that only himself (and possibly Nellie) knew.

Sunday passed quietly. Some of the boys attended one or another of the churches in Ashton, and the Rovers went with them. Dudd Flockley and his cronies took a walk up the river, and reaching a warm, sunny spot, threw themselves down to smoke cigarettes and talk.

"Well, what did you do about the dress-suit case, Jerry?" asked Flockley with a sharp look at his crony.

"Returned it, as you know," was the answer, and Jerry winked suggestively.

"I'd have flung the bag in the river before I would give it to such a chap as Tom Rover," growled Larkspur.

"You trust me, Larky, old boy," answered Jerry Koswell. "I know what I'm doing."

"Humph!"

"I said I returned the case, but I didn't say I returned all that was in it."

"What do you mean by that?" demanded Flockley. "If you've got a secret, out with it."

Koswell looked around to make certain that no outsider was near.

"I kept a few things out of the bag—some things that had Tom Rover's name or his initials on them."

"And you are going to——" went on Flockley.

"I am going to use 'em some day, when I get the chance."

"Good!" cried Flockley. "I'll help you, Jerry!"

"And so will I," added Larkspur. "If we work it right we can get Tom Rover in a peck of trouble."

On Monday morning the college term opened in earnest, and once again the Rovers had to get down to the "grind," as Sam expressed it. But the boys had had a long vacation and were in the best of health, and they did not mind the studying.

"Got to have a good education if you want to get along nowadays," was the way Dick expressed himself. "If you don't learn you are bound to be at the mercy of anybody who wants to take advantage of your ignorance."

"Dick, what are you going to do when you get out of college?" asked Tom.

"I don't know—go into business, I imagine."

"Oh, he'll marry and settle down," chimed in Sam. "He and Dora will live in an ivy-covered cottage like two turtle doves, and——"

Sam got no further, for a pillow thrown by Dick caught him full in the face and made him stagger.

"Sam is thinking of what he and Grace are going to do," said Dick. "And you and Nellie will likely have a cottage across the way," he added, grinning at Tom.

"Really!" murmured Tom, and got as red as a beet. "Say, call it off," he added. "Do you know we have the necktie rush this afternoon?"

"It won't amount to much," answered Sam. "Too many sophs out of it."

"Don't you believe it," said Dick. "Remember, the juniors come into this as well as the sophs."

"Say, I've thought of a plan!" cried Tom. "Greatest ever! I'm going to patent it!" And he commenced to dance around in his excitement.

"What's loose?" asked Songbird, coming up at that moment, followed by some others. "Tom, have you got a pain in your inwards?"

"No, an idea—it's about the same thing," responded Tom gaily. "We want to get the best of the second and third-year fellows during the necktie rush, and I think I know how we can do it. We'll all sew our neckties fast!"

For a moment there was silence, and then, as the others caught the idea, they commenced to laugh.

"That's it!" cried Sam. "I'll sew mine as tight as a drum!"

"I'll rivet mine on, if that will do any good," added Dick.

"Sure thing!" came from Songbird, and he commenced to recite:

"Oh, the sophs and the juniors will try
To steal from the freshies each tie;
  But they will not win,
  For we'll fight them like sin——"

"And bust 'em right plumb in the eye!"

finished Tom. "Oh, say, but will you all sew your neckties fast?"

"Sure!"

"And we'll tell the rest to do so, too," added another freshman who was present.

The news soon circulated, and was kept from all but the first-year students.

It must be confessed that many of the students found it hard to fix their minds on their lessons that afternoon. One boy, Max Spangler, brought on a great laugh when the following question was put to him:

"What great improvement in navigation did Fulton introduce?"

"Neckties," answered Max abstractedly.

"Neckties?" queried the instructor in astonishment.

"I—er—I don't mean neckties," stammered the German-American student, "I mean steamboats."

When the afternoon session was over the students hurried to their various rooms. The sophomores and the juniors who were to take part in the contest talked matters over, and as far as possible laid out a plan of action. It was decided that the largest and heaviest of the second and third-year students were to tackle the smallest freshmen first, while the others were to hold the rest of the first-year men at bay.

"We'll get fifteen or twenty neckties first clip that way," said one of the sophomores, "and it doesn't matter who we get them from. A little chap's tie counts as much as that of a two-hundred pounder."

In the meantime the freshmen were busy following Tom's advice and sewing their ties fast to their collars, shirts, and even their undershirts. Then Dick, who had, unconsciously almost, become a leader, called the boys into an empty recitation-room.

"Now, I've got a plan," said he. "We want to bunch up, and all the little fellows and lightweights get in the center. The heavy fellows can take the outside and fight the others off. Understand?"

"Yes!"

"That's a good idea!"

"Forward to the fray!" yelled Stanley, "and woe be to him who tries to get my tie! His blood be on his own head!" he added tragically.

"Forward!" cried Sam, "and let our watchWord be, 'Die, but no tie!'"

"Now don't get excited," said Dick. "Take it coolly, and I'm certain that when the time is up we'll have the most of our ties still on."

It was the custom to go out on the campus at a given time, and when the chapel bell sounded out the hour Dick led the freshmen forward. They came out of a side door in a body and formed around the flagstaff almost before the sophomores and juniors knew they had appeared.

The seniors took no part, but three had been "told off" to act as referees, and they stood around as if inspecting the buildings and the scenery. The instructors, who also knew what was coming, wisely kept out of sight.

"Come on, and at 'em!" called out Dudd Flockley, and this cry was quickly taken up by all the others who were to take part in the contest.

"Hello! They know a thing or two," said Frank Holden, who was the sophomore leader in the attack. "They've got the little fellows in the middle."

As tightly as possible the freshmen gathered around the flagstaff. Each wore a necktie of the college colors and it was fastened as tightly as strong thread could hold it.

"At 'em!" was the yell of the second and third-year lads. "Tear 'em apart! Pull the ties from 'em!"

And then they leaped in at the big freshmen, and on the instant a battle royal was started. Down went four boys on the campus, rolling over and over. Others caught each other by the hands and shoulders and wrestled valiantly.

Dick and Tom were in the front rank, with Sam directly behind them. Dick was caught by Frank Holden, and the two wrestled with might and main. Frank was big and strong, but Dick managed to hold him so that all the sophomore leader could do was to get his finger tips on the sought-for necktie.

Flockley tackled Tom, and much to his surprise was tripped up and sent flat on his back. Mad with sudden rage, Flockley scrambled up and let out a savage kick for Tom's stomach. But Tom was too quick for the sophomore, and leaped to one side.

"Foul!" cried Tom.

"Don't do that again!" called one of the seniors to Dudd. "If you do you'll be ruled out." Kicking and punching were prohibited by the rules. All the boys could do was to wrestle and throw each other, and either try to pull the neckties away or hold on to them.

On and on the battle waged, each minute growing hotter. Many of the students were almost winded, and felt that they could not endure the struggle much longer. Dick, Tom and Sam managed to keep their neckties, although Sam's was torn loose by two sophomores who held him as in a vise until Stanley came to his assistance. When the time was half up eleven neckties had been captured—two of them almost torn to shreds.

"At 'em!" yelled Frank Holden. "We haven't begun yet!"

"Hold 'em back!" was Dick's rallying answer. "Don't let 'em get near the little fellows!"

Again the contest raged, and this time with increased bitterness. In the melee some few blows were exchanged, but it must be admitted that one side was about as much to blame for this as the other. Three additional neckties were captured, making fourteen in all. As thirty-seven freshmen were in the contest, the sophomores and juniors had to capture five more neckties to win.

"Only three minutes more!" sang out one student, looking at his watch. "At 'em! Rip 'en? apart!"

"Three minutes more!" yelled Dick. "Hold 'em back and we'll win!"

The enemy fought with increased fury, and one more necktie was taken—the collar and collar band coming with it. But then of a sudden the chapel bell tolled out the hour.

"Time's up!" was the cry.

"And we win!" came from a score of freshmen in huge delight.

"Look out! Look out!" cried several small youths in the center of the crowd.

Crack! It was the flagstaff, and all looked in that direction. The pole, old and decayed, was falling. It looked as if it would crush all who stood in its path.

CHAPTER IX

TOM IN TROUBLE

"Look out, the flagpole is coming down!"

"Stand from under, or you'll be killed!"

Crack! came from the pole, and now many saw that it was breaking off close to the ground. Some of the students had clung to it during the contest, and the strain had been too much for the stick, which was much rotted just where it entered the ground.

Those on the outside of the crowd ran away with ease, but not so those who were hemmed in. Two of the smallest of the freshmen, Billy Dean and Charley Atwood, could not move fast enough, and one fell over the other, and both went down.

"Save me!" gasped one of the lads.

"Don't let the pole come down on me!" screamed the other.

The flagstaff was falling swiftly, and Dick and many others saw that it would fall directly across Dean and Atwood unless its progress was stayed.

"Hold it up! Hold it up!" yelled Dick. "Hold it up, or they'll be killed!"

He put up his hands to meet the pole, which was coming down across the front of the campus. Tom did likewise, and so did Frank Hoiden, Stanley Brown, and several others, including an extra tall and powerful senior.

It was a heavy weight, and for the moment the boys under it thought they would have to let it go. Over came the pole, and when it rested on the boys' hands the top overbalanced the bottom and struck the ground, sending the lower end into the air. As this happened Billy Dean and Charley Atwood were hauled out of harm's way. Then the pole was dropped to the campus with a thud.

For several seconds all who stood near were too dazed to speak. Then a cheer arose for those who had held the flagstaff up long enough for the small youths to be rescued.

"Say, that was a close shave!" exclaimed Sam. He, like a good many others, was quite pale.

"It was indeed," said a senior who had come up. "The fellows who held the pole up deserve a good deal of credit."

"Dick Rover suggested it," said Songbird. "Good for you, Dick!" he added warmly.

The falling of the flagstaff sobered the whole party of students, yet the freshmen were jubilant over the fact that they had won in the colors contest.

"And we'll wear the colors this term," cried Tom proudly.

"So we will!" called out others in a chorus. "We'll wear 'em good and strong, too!" And they did. The very next day some of the lads came out with neckties twice the ordinary size, and with hat bands several inches wide, all, of course, in the Brill colors.

Billy Dean and Charley Atwood were much affected by what had occurred, and quickly retired from the scene. But later both of the small students thanked Dick and the others for what had been done for them. The broken flagstaff was hauled away by the laborers of the place, and inside of a week a new pole, much larger than the old one, and set in concrete, was put up.

For several days after the contest over the colors matters ran along smoothly at Brill. The Rover boys made many more friends, and because of his work during the necktie rush Dick was chosen as the leader of the freshmen's class.

"On Friday I am going to fix Tom Rover," said Jerry Koswell to Dudd Flockley, "Just wait and see what I do—and keep your mouth shut."

"I'll keep my mouth shut right enough," answered Dudd, "but what's in the wind?"

"I'm going to pay off Professor Sharp for some of his meanness—and pay off Tom Rover at the same time."

"Give me a map of the proceedings. I'm too tired to guess riddles, Jerry."

"Well, you know how Sharp called me down to-day in English?"

"Sure!"

"Well, I've learned that he just received a new photograph of some lady—I think his best girl. He has it on the mantle in his room. I'm going to doctor that picture, and I'm going to lay the blame on Tom Rover."

"How will you do it?"

"By using something I got out of Rover's dress-suit case."

"Oh, I see!"

"Sharp will suspect Rover at once, because he and Rover had a few words yesterday."

"Good! I hope he catches it well—Rover, I mean," answered Dudd Flockley.

Saturday was more or less of a holiday at Brill, and the three Rover boys planned to go to town. Incidentally, they wished to learn if Dora Stanhope and the Laning girls had as yet arrived at Hope Seminary. They had received io letters from the girls since coming to Brill, and were growing anxious.

Tom was dressing to go to town when there came a knock on his door, and one of the proctors presented himself.

"Thomas Rover, you are wanted at the office immediately," said the man.

"What for?" asked Tom.

"Don't ask me, ask Professor Sharp," answered the proctor, and looked at Tom keenly.

Wondering what could be the matter, Tom finished dressing, and in a few minutes presented himself at the office. President Wallington and Professor Sharp were both waiting for him.

"So you've come at last, have you, you young rascal!" cried Abner Sharp angrily. "How dare you do such an outrageous thing?"

"Gently, professor," remonstrated the presilent of Brill. "You are not yet certain———"

"Oh, he did it, I am sure of it!" spluttered Professor Sharp. "I declare I ought to have him locked up!"

"Did what?" demanded Tom, who was much mystified by what was going on.

"You know well enough, you young reprobate!" stormed the instructor.

"See here, Professor Sharp, I'm neither a rascal nor a reprobate, and I don't want you to call me such!" cried Tom, growing angry himself.

"You are, and I will have you to understand———"

"I am not, and if you call me bad names again I'll—I'll—knock you down!" And Tom doubled tip his fists as he spoke.

"Rover, be quiet!" exclaimed Doctor Wallington, so sternly that both Tom and Professor Sharp subsided. "I'll have no scene in this office. You must behave yourself like a gentleman while you are here. Professor, you must not call a student hard names."

"But this outrage, sir!" spluttered the instructor.

"We'll soon know the truth of the matter."

"I'd like to know what you are talking about," said Tom. "I haven't committed any outrage, so far as I know."

"Didn't you do this?" cried Abner Sharp, and thrust under Tom's nose a photograph of large size. The picture had once represented a fairly good-looking female of perhaps thirty years of age, but now the hair was colored a fiery red, and the end of the nose was of the same hue, while in one corner of the dainty mouth was represented a big cigar, with the smoke curling upward. Under the photograph was scrawled in blue crayon, "Ain't she my darling?"

The representation struck Tom as so comical that he was compelled to laugh outright; he simply couldn't help it. It was just such a joke as he might have played years before, perhaps on old Josiah Crabtree, when at Putnam Hall.

"Ha! So you are even willing to laugh in my face, are you!" almost screamed Abner Sharp, and rushing at Tom he caught the youth and shook him roughly. "Do you—er—know that this lady is my—my affianced wife?"

"Let me go!" cried Tom, and shook himself loose. "Excuse me, sir. I know I hadn't ought to laugh, but it looks so—so awfully funny!" And Tom had to grin again.

"Rover!" broke in the president of Brill sternly, "aren't you ashamed to do such a thing as this?"

"Why—er—what do you mean, sir?"

"Just what I said."

"Oh!" A light began to break in on the fun-loving Rover's mind. "Do you think I did this?"

"Didn't you?"

"Of course he did!" fumed Professor Sharp. "And now he is willing to laugh over his dastardly work!"

"I didn't do it, sir," said Tom firmly.

"You are certain?" It was the head of the college who asked the question.

"Yes, sir. I never saw that picture before."

"But I have the proof against you!" fairly shouted Abner Sharp. "It is useless for you to deny your guilt."

"I say I am not guilty."

"Isn't this your box, Rover?"

As Professor Sharp uttered these words he brought to light a German silver case which Tom had picked up in a curiosity shop in New York. The case had his name engraved on it, and contained pencils, crayons, and other things for drawing.

"Where did you get that?" demanded the youth.

"Never mind where I got it. Isn't it yours?"

"Yes."

"Ha! Do you hear that, Doctor Wallington?" cried Abner Sharp in triumph. "He admits the outfit is his!"

"So I see," said the president of Brill, and if anything his face grew a trifle more stern. "Then you admit your guilt, Rover?" he questioned.

"What! That I defaced the photograph?"

"Yes."

"No, sir! Didn't I say I had never seen the picture before?"

"This photograph was in Professor Sharp's room, on the mantel. The room was locked up, and the professor carried the key. This box was found on the table, beside some books. You had some difficulty with the professor a day or two ago in the classroom."

"I didn't touch the picture, and I haven't been near Professor Sharp's room," answered Tom stoutly. "If I was there, would I be fool enough to leave that box behind, with my name engraved on it? And if the door was locked how would I get in?"

"Did you lend the box to anybody?"

"No. The fact is, I—er—I thought I had left the box home. I—— Oh!"

"Well?"

"I think maybe the box was in my dress-suit case, the case I lost. But it wasn't in the case when it was left at my door that morning."

"Oh, nonsense!" muttered Professor Sharp. "He is guilty, sir, and he might as well own up to it first as last."

"I have told the strict truth!" cried Tom hotly. "I am not in the habit of telling falsehoods."

"Have you any other proof against Rover, Professor Sharp?"

"Not now, but I may be able to pick up more later."

"Hum! This is certainly a serious matter. Rover, you will go to your room and remain there until I send for you again."

"Can't I go down to town?" asked Tom.

"Not for the present. I intend to get to the bottom of this affair, if I possibly can. If you are innocent you shall not suffer. But at present it looks to me as if you were guilty. You may go."

"But, sir——"

"Not another word at present. I have other matters to attend to. I shall call on you later. But remain in your room until I send somebody for you."

An angry answer arose to Tom's lips, but he checked it. In the college Doctor Wallington's word was law, and he knew he would only make matters worse by attempting to argue. With a heavy heart he turned, gazed coldly at Professor Sharp, and left the office.

SONGBIRD MAKES A DISCOVERY

"It's all up with me," said Tom to his brothers when he met them in the hall. "I can't go to town."

"Why not?" asked Sam.

"Got to remain in my room until Doctor Wallington sends for me."

"What have you been doing, Tom?" came from Dick.

"Nothing." And then Tom told of what had occurred in the office. His brothers listened with much interest.

"This is the work of some enemy," said Sam quickly.

"And the one who got hold of the dress-suit case," added Dick. "Tom, do you suspect any one?"

"Only in a general way—Koswell, Flockley, Larkspur, and that crowd."

"It's too bad."

"Say, but that picture was a sight!" cried the fun-loving Rover, and giinned broadly. "No wonder old Sharp was mad. I'd be mad myself, especially if it was a photo of my best girl."

"I hope the doctor doesn't keep you in the room all day," said Sam.

"You and Dick might as well go to town without me," returned Tom with a sigh that he endeavored to suppress. "Your staying here won't do me any good."

"What will you do?"

"Oh, read or study. It will give me a chance to catch up in my Latin. I was a bit rocky in that yesterday. I can bone away until the president sends a special message for me."

"Want us to get anything for you?" questioned Dick.

"Yes, a good fat letter from—well, a fat letter, that's all."

"Postmarked Cedarville, and in Nellie Laning's handwriting," came from Sam slyly.

"I didn't know they postmarked letters in handwriting," answered Tom innocently.

"Oh, you know what I mean."

"Sure, Sam, for I know you're looking for a letter, too. Well, run along, children, and play," said Tom, and a minute later Sam and Dick set off for Ashton.

Tom did not feel as lighthearted as his words would seem to indicate. He knew that the charge against him was a serious one, and he saw no way of clearing himself. The finding of the box with his name on it seemed to be proof positive against him.

"No use of talking, the minute I get to school I seem to get into trouble," he soliloquized. "Wonder if they'll put me in a cell, like old Crabtree did at Putnam Hall? If they do I'll raise a kick, sure as eggs are unhatched chickens!"

Tom sat down to study, but he could not fix his mind on his lessons. Then he heard somebody come along the hallway and turn into the next room.

"Must be Songbird, or else one of the servants," he thought. "Guess I'll take a look." If it was Songbird, he could chat with his friend for a while.

He went to the next room. As he opened the door he saw Songbird, with his back toward him. The so-styled poet was waving his arms in the air and declaiming:

"The weeping winds were whispering through the wood,
☐The rolling rill ran 'round the ragged rock;
The shepherd, with his sunny, smiling face,
☐Was far away to feed his flitting flock.
Deep in the dingle, dank and dark——"

"I thought I heard an old crow bark!"

 finished Tom. "Say, Songbird, how much is that poetry by the yard—or do you sell it by the ton?" he went on.

At the sound of Tom's voice the would-be poet gave a start. But he quickly recovered. He scowled for a moment and then took on a look of resignation.

"You'v spoiled one of the best thoughts I ever had," he said.

"Don't you believe it, Songbird," answered Tom. "I've heard you make up poetry worth ten times that. Don't you remember that litthe sonnet you once composed, entitled 'Who Put Ink in Willie's Shoes?' It was great, grand, sublime!"

"I never wrote such a sonnet!" cried Songbird. "Ink in shoes, indeed! Tom, you don't know real poetry when you see it!"

"That's a fact, I don't. But, say, what's on the carpet, as the iceman said to the thrush?"

"Nothing. I thought I'd write a few verses, that's all. Thought you were going to town with Sam and Dick?"

"Can't." And once again Tom had to tell his story. He had not yet finished when Songbird gave an exclamation.

"It fits in!" he cried.

"Fits in? What?" asked Tom.

 "What I heard a while ago."

"What did you hear?"

"Heard Flockley, Koswell and Larkspur talking together. Koswell said he had fixed you, and that you were having a bad half hour with the president."

"Where was this?"

"In the library. I was in an alcove, and they didn't see me. I was busy reading some poetry by Longfellow—fine thing—went like this——"

"Never mind. Chop out the poetry now, Songbird. What more did they say?"

"Nothing. They walked away, and I—er—I got so interested in making up verses I forgot all about it until now."

"I wish you had heard more. Do you know where they went to?"

"No, but I can look around if you want me to."

"I wish very much that you would. I can't leave, or I'd go myself."

A few more words followed, and then Songbird went off to hunt up the Flockley crowd. On the campus he met Max Spangler.

"Yes, I saw them," said the German-American student in answer to a question. "They are down along the river, just above the boathouse."

"Thank you."

"I'll show you if you want me to," went on Max.

"You might come along, if you have nothing else to do," answered Songbird.

The two walked toward the river, and after a few minutes espied Flockley and the others sitting on some rocks, in the sun, talking earnestly.

"I want to hear what they are saying," said Songbird. "I have a special reason." And at Max's look of surprise he told something of what had happened.

"If Koswell is that mean he ought to be exposed," said Max. "I don't blame him for playing a trick on old Sharp, but to lay the blame on Tom why, that's different."

"Will you come along?"

"If you want me to."

"I don't want to drag you into trouble, Max."

"I dink I can take care of myself," answered the German-American student.

The pair passed around to the rear of the spot where Flockley and his cronies were located. Here was a heavy clump of brushwood, so they were able to draw quite close without being seen.

The talk was of a general character for a while, embracing football and other college sports, and Songbird was disappointed. But presently Jerry Koswell began to chuckle.

"I can't help but think of the way I put it over Tom Rover," he exclaimed. "I'll wager old Sharp will make him suffer good and proper."

"Maybe they'll suspend Rover," said Bart Larkspur. "But that would be carrying it pretty far, wouldn't it?"

"They won't suspend him, but he'll surely be punished," came from Dudd Flockley. "By the way, are you sure it was a photo of Sharp's best girl?"

"Yes; but she isn't a girl, she's a woman, and not particularly good-looking at that," answered Jerry Koswell.

"Well, Sharp isn't so very handsome," answered Larkspur. "His nose is as sharp as his name."

"I suppose Rover will wonder how somebody got hold of that case of pencils and crayons," remarked Flockley. "If he——"

"Hello, Max!" cried a voice from behind the bushes, and the next moment a stout youth landed on Max Spangler's back, carrying him down with a crash in the brushwood. "What are you doing here, anyway?"

At the interruption the whole Flockley crowd started to their feet, and turning, beheld not only Max and the boy who had come up so suddenly, but also Songbird. The latter was nearest to them, and Koswell eyed him with sudden suspicion.

"What are you doing here?" he demanded, while Max and his friend were wrestling in a good-natured way in the bushes.

"Oh, I've been listening to some interesting information," answered Songbird.

"Playing the eavesdropper, eh?" came from Flockley with a sneer.

"If so, it was for a good purpose," answered the would-be poet warmly.

"Say, Jerry, you want to look out for him!" cried Larkspur warningly. "He rooms with Dick Rover, remember. They are old chums."

"I know that," said Koswell. He faced Songbird again. "How long have you been here?" he cried angrily.

"That is my business, Koswell. But I heard enough of your talk to know how you tried to put Tom Rover in a hole. It's a mean piece of business, and it has got to be stopped."

"Bah!"

"You can 'bah!' all you please, but I mean what I say. To play a joke is one thing, to blame it on a fellow student who is innocent is another. As the poet Shelley says— But what's the use of wasting poetry on a chap like you? Max, you heard what was said, didn't you?"

By this time the German-American student was free of his tormentor, a happy-go-lucky student named Henry Cale. He nodded to Songbird.

"Yes, I heard it," he said, and gave Koswell a meaning look.

"Fine business to be in, listening around corners," sneered Larkspur.

"Say that once more and I'll punch your head!" cried Max, doubling up his fists.

"What are you fellows going to do?" questioned Koswell. He was beginning to grow alarmed.

"That depends on what you fellows do," returned Songbird.

"Why—er—do you think I am going to the doctor and—er—confess?"

"You have got to clear Tom Rover."

"Our word is as good as yours," said Larkspur.

"Then you are willing to tell a string of falsehoods, eh?" said Songbird coldly.

"I didn't say so."

"But you meant it. Well, Larkspur, it won't do. I know about this, and so does Max. Koswell has got to clear Tom Rover, and that is all there is to it."

"Will you keep quiet about me if I clear Rover?" asked Jerry Koswell eagerly.

"That depends on what Tom Rover says. I am going right to him now and tell him what I heard."

"And I'll go along," said Max. He turned to Henry Cale. "You will have to excuse me, Henry. This is a private affair of importance."

"Sure," was the ready answer. "I wouldn't have butted in if I had known something was doing," and Henry walked off toward the college buildings.

"Just tell Tom Rover to wait—we'll fix it up somehow," cried Jerry to Songbird and Max as the pair departed. "It's all a—er—a mistake. I'm—er—sorry I got Rover into it—really I am."

"No doubt of it, now!" answered Songbird significantly. "Evildoers are usually sorry—after they are caught!"

CHAPTER XI

HOW TOM ESCAPED PUNISHMENT

Dick and Sam were good walkers, so it did not take them long to reach Ashton. While covering the distance they talked over Tom's dilemma, but failed to reach any conclusion concerning it.

"It's too bad," said Sam, "especially when the term has just opened. It will give Tom a black. eye."

"I don't think he'll stand for too much punishment, being innocent, Sam. He'll go home first."

"I was thinking of that. But we don't want to be here with Tom gone."

Arriving at Ashton, the boys hurried to the post-office. The mail for the college was in, and among it they found several letters from home and also epistles from Dora Stanhope and the Laning girls.

"Here's one for Tom—that will cheer him up a bit," said Dick, holding up one addressed in Nellie Laning's well-known hand.

The boys sat down in an out-of-the-way corner to read their letters. Dick had a communication of ten pages from Dora, and Sam had one of equal length from Grace. Then there was one for all the boys from their father, and another from their Aunt Martha.

"The girls are coming next Wednesday," said Dick. "I hope we can get down to the depot when they arrive."

"Don't forget poor Tom, Dick."

"Yes. Isn't it too bad?"

"Nellie will cry her eyes out if he is sent away."

"Oh, we've got to fix that up somehow."

Having read the letters carefully, the boys went to one of the stores to make some purchases, and then drifted down to the depot. A train was coming in, but they did not expect to see anybody they knew. As a well-dressed young man, carrying a suit case, alighted, both gave an exclamation:

"Dan Baxter!"

The individual they mentioned will need no introduction to my old readers. During their days at Putnam Hall the Rover boys had had in Dan Baxter and his father enemies who had done their best to ruin them. The elder Baxter had repented after Dick had done him a great service, but Dan had kept up his animosity until the Rovers imagined he would be their enemy for life. But at last Dan, driven to desperation by the actions of those with whom he was associating, had also repented, and it was the Rovers who had set him on his feet again. They had loaned him money, and he had gotten a position as a traveling salesman for a large wholesale house. How he was faring they did not know, since they had not seen or heard of him for a long time.

"Hello! You here?" cried Dan Baxter, and dropped his suit case on the depot platform. "Thought you were at the college."

"Came down for an airing," answered Dick. He held out his hand. "How goes it with you, Dan?"

"Fine! Couldn't be better." Baxter shook hands with both boys, and they could not help but notice how clean-cut and happy he appeared, quite in contrast to the careless, sullen Dan of old.

"Come on business?" inquired Sam.

"Yes."

"What are you selling?" asked Dick.

"I am in the jewelry line now, representing one of the biggest houses in the United States. I was going through to Cleveland, but I made up my mind to stop off here and see you. I heard from one of the old boys that you were here."

"I am sure I am glad to see you, Dan," said Dick, "and glad to know you are doing well."

"Maybe you'll be a member of the firm some day," added Sam with a smile.

"I don't know about that. I'm willing to work, and the traveling suits me first-rate. They pay me a good salary, too—thirty dollars per week and all expenses."

"Good enough!" cried Dick.

"I came to see you fellows," went on Dan Baxter in a lower voice. "I haven't forgotten what you did for me when I was on my uppers. It was splendid of you. I realize it more every day I live. My father is with me now—that is, when I'm home. We are happier than we ever were before."

"That's good," murmured Sam.

"I want to see you all. Where is Tom?"

"Up to the college." Sam did not deem it necessary to go into particulars.

"I'd like to see him, too. I've got something each of you."

"What is that?"

"Before I tell you I want you to promise you'll accept it. And by the way, you got that money back, didn't you?"

"Yes."

"Well, will you accept what I want to give you? I want to show you I appreciate your kindness."

"We didn't expect anything, Dan," said Dick.

"Oh, I know that, Dick, but please say you'll take what I have for you. It isn't so very much, but it's something."

"All right, if you want it that way," answered the oldest Rover, seeing that his former enemy was very much in earnest.

Dan Baxter put his hand in an inner pocket and brought forth three small packages.

"This is for you, Dick, and this for you, Sam," he said. "The other is for Tom. They are all alike."

The two Rovers undid the packages handed to them. Inside were small jewelry cases, and each contained a beautiful stickpin of gold, holding a ruby with three small diamonds around it.

"Say, this is fine!" murmured Sam.

"Dan, we didn't expect this," said Dick.

"But you said you'd accept," pleaded Baxter. "They are all alike, as I said before. I had the firm make them to order, so there is nothing else like them on the market. The three diamonds represent you three brothers, and the ruby—well, when you look at that you can think of me, if you want to. And another thing," went on Baxter, his face flushing a trifle, "the pins are settled for. They didn't come out of my stock. I mention this because—because——" The young traveling salesman stopped in some confusion.

"Dan, we know you are not that kind," said Dick hastily.

"Well, I was, but I'm not that kind any longer—everything I do is as straight as a string. I paid for those stickpins out of my wages. I hope you will all wear them."

"I certainly shall," said Dick. "I shall prize this gift very highly."

"And so shall I," added Sam.

Dan Baxter had heard something about their search for the fortune on Treasure Isle, and as they walked over to the hotel for lunch the Rovers gave him some of the details. In return he told them of some of his experiences on the road while representing a carpet house and another concern, as well as the jewelry manufacturers. He told them of several of the former pupils of Putnam Hall, including Fenwick, better known as Mumps, who he said was novr working in a Chicago hotel.

"You boys can rest assured of one thing," said Dan Baxter during the course of the conversation, "if I can ever do you a good turn I'll do it, no matter what it costs me."

"That is very kind to say, Dan," answered Dick. "And let me say, if we can do anything more for you we'll do it."

The three youths spent several hours together and then Sam and Dick said they would have to get back to college. Secretly they were worried about Tom.

"Well, please give the pin to Tom," said Baxter, "and if you feel like it, write me a letter some day," and he told them of the cities he expected to visit during his next selling tour. Then the Rovers and their one-time enemy separated.

"Not at all like the old Dan Baxter," was Sam's comment.

"He is going to make a fine business man, after all," returned Dick. "Well, I am glad of it, and glad, too, that he and his father are reconciled to each other."

Sam and Dick had covered about half the distance back to Brill when they saw a figure striding along the country road at a rapid gait.

"Why, say, that looks like Tom!" cried Sam.

"It is Tom," returned his big brother.

"Do you suppose he has run away?"

"I don't know. Perhaps the doctor has suspended him."

"Hello!" called Tom as he came closer. "Thought I'd find you in town yet. Come on back and have some fun."

"What does this mean, Tom?" demanded Dick, coming to a halt in front of his brother. He saw at a glance that Tom looked rather happy.

"What does what mean, my dear Richard?" asked the fun-loving Rover in a sweet, girlish voice.

"You know well enough. Did you run away?"

"No. Walked away."

"Without permission?" asked Sam.

"My dear Samuel, you shock me!" cried Tom in that same girlish voice.

"See here, let us in on the ground floor of the Sphinx," cried Dick impatiently.

"I will, kind sirs," answered Tom, this time in a deep bass voice. "I went to the room and remained there about an hour. Songbird went out on a still hunt, Max with him. The two overheard Jerry Koswell and his cronies talking, learned Jerry did the trick, came back and told me, and——"

"You told the president," finished Sam.

"Not on your collar button," answered Tom. "I waited. The president sent for me. I went. He tried to get me to confess, and then the telephone rang, and that did the biz."

"Say, Tom, are you crazy?" demanded Dick.

"Crazy? Yes, I'm crazy with joy. Who wouldn't be to get free so easily?"

"But explain it," begged Sam.

"I can't explain it. As I said, the president tried to make me confess, and of course I had nothing to confess. When the telephone rang I heard one voice and then two others, one after another. I think they belonged to Koswell, Flockley and Larkspur, but I am not sure. The voices talked to Doctor Wallington about ten minutes. He got mad at first and then calmed down. I heard him ask, 'In Professor Sharp's room?' and somebody said 'Yes.' Four times he asked for names, but I don't think he got them. Then he went out of the office and was gone about a quarter of an hour. When he returned he said, 'Now, on your honor, for the last time, Rover, did you mar that photograph?' and I said 'No,' good and hard. Then he said he believed me, and was sorry he had suspected me, and he added that I could go off for the rest of the day and enjoy myself, and here I am."

"And you didn't squeal on Koswell & Company?" asked Sam.

"Nary a squeal."

"Do you imagine they confessed?"

"I think they told the president over the 'phone that I was innocent, maybe the three swore to it, but I don't think they gave their names."

"What did they mean about Sharp's room?"

"I was curious about that, and I found out from one of the servants. Sharp found an envelope under the door. It contained a five-dollar bill, and on it was written in a scrawl, 'For a new photograph.'"

"Koswell & Company got scared mightily," mused Dick. "Well, I am glad, Tom, that you are out of it."

"And as a token of your escape we'll present you with this," added Sam, and brought forth the package from Dan Baxter. Tom was much surprised, and listened to the story about the former bully of Putnam Hall with interest.

"Good for Dan!" he cried. "I'll write him a letter the first chance I get."

"And here's a letter from Nellie," said Dick, "and one from father, and another from Aunt Martha."

"Hurrah! That's the best yet!" exclaimed Tom. "I've got to read 'em all. Sit down and rest." And he dropped down on a grassy bank and his brothers followed suit.

CHAPTER XII

IN WHICH THE GIRLS ARRIVE

"You may be sure of one thing, Torn," remarked Dick while he and his brothers were walking back to Brill, some time later, "Jerry Koswell has it in for you. You had better watch him closely."

"I intend to do so," answered Tom. "But there is another thing which both of you seem to have forgotten. That's about the dress-suit case. Did Koswell find it, and if so, did he take anything else besides the box of pencils and crayons?"

"He'll never admit it," put in Sam. "Not unless you corner him, as Songbird did about the photo."

"He'll have to tell where he got the box, Sam."

"I doubt if you get any satisfaction."

And Sam was right, as later events proved. When Tom tackled Koswell the latter said positively that he knew nothing of the dress-suit case. He said he had found the box on a stand in the hallway near Professor Sharp's door, and had used it because it suited his purpose.

"But you saw it had my name on it," said Tom.

"No, I didn't. It was rather dark in the hall, and all I saw was that it contained pencils and crayons," answered Jerry Koswell.

"Well, I don't believe you," answered Tom abruptly. "You did it on purpose, and maybe some day I'll be able to prove it." And he walked off, leaving Koswell in anything but a comfortable frame of mind.

Tom was curious to see how Professor Sharp would act after the affair. During the first recitation the instructor seemed ill at ease, but after that he acted as usual. Tom half suspected the professor still thought him guilty.

"Well, it was a pretty mean thing to do," soliloquized the fun-loving Rover. "If anybody did that to a picture of Nellie I'd mash him into a jelly."

All of the Rovers were awaiting the arrival of the girls with interest, and each was fearful that some poor recitation might keep him from going to meet them at the Ashton depot on Wednesday. But, luckily, all got permission to go to town, and they started without delay as soon as the afternoon session was ended.

"Where bound?" asked Songbird, in some surprise, as he saw them driving off in a carriage Dick had ordered by telephone.

"Going to meet Dora and Nellie and Grace," answered Dick. "Do you—er—want to come along?"

"Oh, sure. I'll see them all home myself," answered the would-be poet with a wink of his eye. "No, thank you. I know enough to keep out of somebody else's honey pot. Give them my regards," he added, and strolled off, murmuring softly:

"If thou love me as I love thee,
How happy thee and I will be!"

The boys got down to the depot ahead of time, and were then told that the train was fifteen minutes late. They put in the time as best they could, although every minute seemed five.

"Hello! There is Dudd Flockley!" exclaimed Sam presently, and pointed to the dudish student, who was crossing the street behind the depot.

"Maybe he came down to meet somebody, too," said Tom. "More than likely there will be quite a bunch of girls bound for the seminary."

At last the train rolled in, and the three Rovers strained their eyes to catch the first sight of their friends.

"There they are!" shouted Dick, and pointed to a parlor car. He ran forward, and so did his brothers. The porter was out with his box, but it was the boys who assisted the girls to alight, and Dick who tipped the knight of the whisk-broom.

"Here at last!" cried Dick. "We are so glad you've come!"

"Thought the train would never get here," added Sam.

"Longest wait I've had since I was able to walk," supplemented Tom.

"Oh, Tom, you big tease!" answered Nellie merrily, and caught him by both hands.

"Yes, we are late," said Dora a bit soberly. She gave Dick's hand a tight squeeze. They looked at each other, and on the instant he saw that she had something to tell him.

"How long it seems since we saw you last," said Grace as she took Sam's hand. Then there was handshaking all around, and all the girls and boys tried to speak at once, to learn how the others had been since they had separated after the treasure hunt.

"We'll have to look after our trunks," said Dora. "There they are," and she pointed to where they had been dumped on a truck.

"I'll take care of the baggage," said Tom. "Just give me the checks."

"And we've got to find a carriage to take us to Hope," added Grace.

"All arranged," answered Sam. "We are going to take you up. Dick is going to take Dora in a buggy, and Tom and I are going to take you and Nellie in a two-seated. The baggage can go in a wagon behind."

"But I thought there was a seminary stage," began Grace.

"There is, and if you'd rather take it——"

"Oh, no! The carriage ride will be much nicer." And Grace looked at Sam in a manner that made his heart beat much faster than before.

"Do you know, it seems awfully queer to be rich and to be going to a fine boarding school," said Nellie. "I declare, I'm not used to it yet. But I'm glad on papa and mamma's account, for neither of them have to work as hard as they did."

"Papa is going to improve the farm fully," said Grace. "He is going to put up a new barn and a carriage house and a new windmill for pumping water, and he has bought a hundred acres from the farm in the back, and added, oh, I don't know how many more cows. And we've got a splendid team of horses, and the cutest pony you ever saw. And next year he is going to rebuild the wing of the house and put on a big piazza., where we can have rocking-chairs and a hammock——"

"Yum! yum!" murmured Sam. "The hammock for mine, when I call."

"Built for two, I suppose," remarked Dick dryly.

"Dick Rover!" cried Grace, and blushed.

"He'll want it for himself and Dor——" began Sam.

"Here comes Tom," interrupted Dick hastily. "All right about the baggage?" he asked loudly.

"All right. The trunks and cases will go to the seminary inside of an hour," answered Tom, "so we might as well be off ourselves. We can drive slowly, you know."

"Well, you can go ahead and set the pace," answered his elder brother.

The buggy and the carriage were already on hand, and soon the boys and girls were in the turnouts, and Tom drove off, with Dick following. As they did so they saw Dudd Flockley standing near, eyeing them curiously. They had to drive close to the dudish student, who was attired in his best, and he stared boldly at Dora and the Laning girls.

"What a bold young man!" was Dora's comment after they had passed.

"He's a student at Brill," answered Dick. "Not a very nice kind, either." Dick was much put out, for he did not like any young man to stare at Dora.

Ashton was soon left behind, and carriage and buggy bowled along slowly over a country road lined on either side with trees and bushes and tidy farms. Under the trees Dick allowed his horse to drop into a walk, and managed to drive with one hand while the other found Dora's waist and held it.

"Dick, somebody might see you!" she half whispered.

"Well, I can't help it, Dora," he answered. "It's been such a long time since we met."

"Yes, it seems like years and years, doesn't it?"

"And to think we've got to go through college before-before we can——"

"Yes, but Dick, isn't it splendid that we are going to be so close to each other? Why, we'll be able to meet lots of times!"

"If the seminary authorities will let you. I understand they are very strict."

"Oh, well, we'll meet anyhow, won't we?"

"If you say so, dear."

"Why, yes, dear—that is—— Oh, now see what you've done!—knocked my hat right down on my ear! Now, you mustn't—one is enough! Just suppose another carriage should come up—with somebody in it from the seminary?"

"I've got my eye open," answered Dick. "But just one more—and then you can fix your hat. They've got to make some allowance for folks that are engaged," he added softly, as he pressed her cheek close to his own.

"Are we engaged, Dick?" she asked as she adjusted her hat.

"Aren't we?" he demanded. "Why, of course we are!"

"Well, if you say so, but—but—I suppose some folks would think we were rather young."

"Well, I'm not so young as I used to be—and I'm growing older every day."

"So am I. I am not near as young as I was when we first met—on that little steamboat on Cayuga Lake, when you and Tom and Sam were going to Putnam Hall for the first time."

"No, you're not quite so young, Dora, but you are just as pretty. In fact, you're prettier than ever."

"Oh, you just say that!"

"I mean it, and I'm the happiest fellow in the world this minute," cried Dick, and caught her again in his arms. Once more the hat went over on Dora's ear, but this time she forgot to mention it. Truth to tell, for the time being she was just as happy as he was.

But presently her face grew troubled, and he remembered the look she had given him at the depot.

"Something is on your mind, Dora," he said. "What is it?"

"Dick, do you know that Tad Sobber is alive? That he escaped from that dreadful hurricane in West Indian waters?"

"Yes, I know it. But I didn't know it until a few days ago, when Songbird Powell came to Brill. He said he had met Sobber in Ithaca."

"He came to see mamma."

"I was afraid he would. What did he say?"

"He came one evening, after supper. It was dark and stormy, and he drove up in a buggy. Mamma and I and the servants were home alone, although Nellie had been over in the afternoon. He rang the bell, and asked for mamma, and the girl ushered him into the parlor. He asked the girl if we had company, and he said if we had he wouldn't bother us."

"Guess he was afraid of being arrested."

"Perhaps so. He told the girl he was a friend from New York. I went down first, and when I saw him I was almost scared to death. I thought I was looking at a ghost."

"Naturally, since you thought he had been drowned. It's too bad he scared you so, Dora."

"He said he had come on business, and without waiting began to talk about the treasure we had taken from the isle. He insisted upon it that the treasure belonged to him, since his uncle, Sid Merrick, was dead. When my mother came in he demanded that she give him some money and sign some papers."

"What did your mother do?"

"She refused, of course. Then he got very wild and talked in a rambling fashion. Oh, Dick, I am half inclined to think he is crazy!" And Dora shuddered

"What did he say after your mother refused to do as he wished?"

"He got up and walked around the parlor, waving his hands and crying that we were robbing him, that the treasure was his, and that the Rovers were nothing but thieves. Then mamma ordered him out of the house and sent the girl to get the man who runs the farm for us. But before the man came Sobber went away, driving his horse as fast as he could."

"Have you heard from him since?"

"Yes. The next day we got an unsigned letter. In it Sobber said that, by hook or by crook, he intended to get possession of the treasure, and for the Rovers to beware."

"BUMPED FAIRLY AND SQUARELY INTO THE CRAFT."—*Page* 134.

The Rover Boys at College.

CHAPTER XIII

THE ROWING RACE

Having told so much, Dora went into all the particulars of Tad Sobber's visit to the Stanhope homestead. She told of how Sobber had argued, and she said he had affirmed that the Rovers had falsified matters so that the Stanhopes and the Lanings might benefit thereby.

"What he says is absolutely untrue," said Dick. "Father went over those papers with care, and so did the lawyers, and the treasure belongs to you and the Lanings, and to nobody else."

"Don't you think Sid Merrick fooled Sobber?" asked the girl.

"Perhaps, but I guess Tad was willing to be fooled. They set their hearts on that money, and now Tad can't give it up. In one way I am sorry for him, and if a small amount of cash would satisfy him and set him on his feet, I'd hand it over. We put Dan Baxter on his feet that way."

"Oh, but Baxter isn't Sobber, Dick. Sobber is wild and wicked. I was so afraid he would attack mamma and me I hardly knew what to do. And his eyes rolled so when he talked!"

"Did he go to the Lanings?"

"No."

"Probably he was afraid of your uncle. Mr. Laning won't stand for any nonsense. I suppose your mother is afraid he'll come back?"

"Yes; and to protect herself she has hired one of the farm men to sleep in the house. The man was once in the army, and he knows how to use a gun."

"Then that will make Sobber keep his distance. He is a coward at heart. I found that out when we went to Putnam Hall together."

"But you must beware of him, Dick. He may show himself here next."

"It won't do him any good. All I've got here is a little spending money. No, I don't think he'll show himself here. More than likely he'll try to hire some shyster lawyer to fight for the treasure in the courts. But I don't think he'll be able to upset your claim."

They had now reached Hope Seminary, and the conversation came to an end. The boys helped the girls to alight, and said good-by. Then they drove back to Ashton, where the buggy was left at the livery stable, and all piled into the carriage for the college. On the way Dick told his brothers about Tad Sobber.

"Dora is right. He is a bad egg," said Sam. "I wouldn't trust him under any consideration."

"He is too much of a coward to attack anybody openly," was Tom's comment. "But as Dick says, he may hire some shyster lawyer to take the matter into the courts. It would be too bad if the fortune was tied up in endless litigation."

"He's got to get money to fight with first," said Dick.

"Oh, some lawyers will take a case like that on a venture."

"That's true."

Several days passed quietly, and the Rover boys applied themselves diligently to their studies, for they wished to make fine records at Brill.

"We are here to get a good education," was the way Dick expressed himself, "and we want to make the most of our time."

"As if I wasn't boning away to beat the band!" murmured Tom reproachfully.

"I'd like to take the full course in about two years," came from Sam.

"College studies are mighty hard," broke in Songbird, who was working over his chemistry. "I don't get any chance to write poetry any more."

"For which let us all be truly thankful," murmured Sam to Tom.

"Ten minutes more," announced Dick, looking at his watch. "Then what do you say to a row on the river?"

"Suits me!" cried Tom.

"All right, then. Now clear out, and—silence!"

A quarter of an hour later the Rover boys and Songbird walked down to the river. There were plenty of boats to be had, and Dick and Tom were soon out. Songbird and Sam received an invitation to go for a ride in a gasolene launch owned by Stanley.

"Suits me!" cried the would-be poet. "I can row any time, but I can't always ride in a motor boat."

"Same here," said Sam. A number of craft were on the river, including one containing Jerry Koswell and Bart Larkspur. Koswell scowled as he saw Tom and Dick rowing near by.

"We'll give 'em a shaking up," he said to his crony, and turned their rowboat so that it bumped fairly and squarely into the craft manned by Tom and Dick. The shock was so great that Dick, who had gotten up to fix his seat, was nearly hurled overboard.

"See here, what do you mean by running into us?" demanded the oldest Rover on recovering his balance.

"Sorry, but it couldn't be helped," answered Koswell. "Why didn't you get out of the way?"

"We didn't have to," retorted Sam, "and if you try that trick again somebody will get his head punched."

"Talk is cheap," sneered Larkspur.

"Say, I heard you fellows have been boasting of how you can row," went on Koswell after a pause.

"We haven't been boasting, but we can row," answered Tom.

"Want to race?"

"When?"

"Now."

"I don't know as I care to race with a chap like you, Koswell," answered Dick pointedly.

"You're afraid."

"No, I am not afraid."

"Let us race them," whispered Tom to his brother. "I am not afraid of them."

"Oh, neither am I. Tom."

"We'll race you to Rock Island and back," said Koswell, after consulting Larkspur.

"All right," answered Dick.

"Want to bet on the result?" questioned Koswell. He was usually willing to bet on anything.

"We don't bet," answered Tom.

"And we wouldn't with you, if we did," added Dick. "I don't think you are in our class, Koswell, and you never will be. At the same time, since you are so anxious to row against us, we'll race you—and beat you."

This answer enraged Jerry Koswell, and he dared the Rovers to wager ten dollars on the race. They would not, but others took up the bet, and then several other wagers were made.

Rock Island was a small, stony spot half a mile up the stream, so the race would be about a mile in length. Frank Holden was chosen as referee and umpire, and all of the contestants prepared for the struggle.

"Your boat is lighter than that of the Rovers," said Holden to Koswell and Larkspur. "You really ought to give them some lead."

"No. This is an even start," growled Koswell.

"Very well, but it doesn't seem quite fair."

It was soon noised around that the race was to take place, and the river bank speedily became lined with students anxious to see how the contest would terminate.

"Now, Tom, take it easy at the start, but finish up strong," cautioned Dick.

"I feel like pulling a strong stroke from the first," answered Tom. "Let us do it, and leave them completely in the shade."

"No. We must first try to find out what they can do."

"Say, you've got to beat 'em," came from Sam, as the launch came close. "If they win you'll never hear the end of it."

"They're not going to win," answered Dick, quietly but firmly.

"All ready?" asked Frank Holden, as the boats drew up side by side near the boathouse float.

"We are!" sang out Tom.

"Ready!" answered Jerry Koswell.

"Go!" shouted Frank.

Four pairs of oars dropped into the water simultaneously, and away shot the two craft side by side. There was no disguising the fact that Koswell and Larkspur were good oarsmen, and what was equally important, they had done much practicing together. On the other hand, while Dick and Tom could row well, they had pulled together but twice since coming to Brill.

"You've got your work cut out for you!" shouted Songbird. "But never mind. Go in and win!"

For the first quarter of a mile the two rowboats kept close together. Occasionally one would forge ahead a few indies, but the other would speedily overtake it. Then, however, the Rover boys settled down to a strong, steady stroke, and forged a full length ahead.

"See! see! The Rovers are winning!" shouted Max in delight.

"That's the way to do it!" cried Stanley. "Keep it up! You're doing nobly!"

"Show 'em the way home!" added Songbird.

"Pull, Jerry! Pull!, Bart!" screamed Dudd Flockley to his cronies. "Don't let them beat you!"

Before long the island was reached, and the Rovers rounded it a length and a half ahead. This made Jerry Koswell frantic, and he called on Larkspur to increase the stroke.

"All right, I'm with you," was the short answer.

The increase in the stroke speedily told, and inch by inch the second boat began to overhaul the first. Then Tom made a miss, sending a shower of water into the air. At this the craft containing Koswell and Larkspur shot ahead.

"Hurrah! That's the way to do it!" yelled Flockley in delight. "Even money on the green boat!"

"Take you," answered Spud Jackson promptly. "How much?"

"A fiver."

"All right."

"Steady, Tom," cautioned Dick. "Now, then. Ready?"

"Yes."

"Then bend to it. One, two, three, four."

Again the Rover boys went at the rowing with a will, increasing their stroke until it was six to the minute more than that of Koswell and Larkspur. The latter were frantic, and tried to do likewise, but found it impossible. Inch by inch the Rovers' craft went ahead. Now it was half a length, then a length, then two lengths.

"Say, there is rowing for you!" was the comment of a senior. "Just look at them bend to it!"

"Yes, and look at the quick recovery," added another fourth-year student.

From two lengths the Rovers went three lengths ahead. Then Koswell missed a stroke, and tumbled up against Larkspur.

"Hi! What are you doing?" spluttered Larkspur in disgust.

"Cou—couldn't hel—help it," panted Jerry. He was all but winded, for the pulling had been too much for him.

"The Rovers win! The Rovers win!" was the shout that went up, and in the midst of the hubbub Dick and Tom crossed the line, winning by at least six lengths. Koswell and Larkspur were so disgusted that they did not even finish, but stopped rowing and turned away from the float.

"The Rovers win," announced Frank Holden. "A fine race, too," he added. "Let me congratulate you," and he waved his hand pleasantly to Dick and Tom.

"I got a pain in my side, and that made me miss the stroke," said Jerry Koswell lamely. "Some day I'll race them again, and win, too."

"You should have won this time," growled Dudd Flockley when he was alone with his cronies. "I dropped twenty dollars on that race."

"I never thought they could row like that," was Larkspur's comment. "I don't think I want to row against them again."

Dick and Tom were warmly congratulated by all their friends. It had been a well-earned victory, and they were correspondingly happy. Koswell was sourer than ever against them, and vowed he would "square up" somehow, and Larkspur agreed to help him. Dudd Flockley was glum, for his spending money for the month was running low, and it was going to be hard to pay the wagers he had lost.

CHAPTER XIV

WILLIAM PHILANDER TUBBS

On the following Saturday the Rover boys went down to Ashton in the afternoon. They had arranged for the hire of a large touring car, with a competent chauffeur, and were to take Dora and the Laning girls out for a ride to another town called Toddville. Here they were to have supper at the hotel, returning to Ashton in the evening.

Lest it be thought strange that the girls could get permission from the seminary authorities to absent themselves, let me state that matters had been explained by Mrs. Stanhope and Mrs. Laning to the principal of Hope, so Dora and her cousins were free to go out with the Rovers whenever they could go out at all.

"We'll have the best time ever!" cried Tom enthusiastically. "I hope you ordered a fine supper over the telephone, Dick."

"I did," was the reply. "Just the things I know the girls like."

"And a bouquet of flowers," added Sam. He knew that Grace loved flowers.

"Yes. I didn't forget them, Sam."

The boys arrived in Ashton a little ahead of time, and while waiting for the chauffeur of the car to appear they walked down to the depot to see if there would be any new arrivals on the Saturday special.

When the train pulled into the depot a tall, well-dressed youth, with an elaborate dress-suit case and a bag of golf sticks, descended from the parlor car and gazed around him wonderingly.

"Are you—ah—sure this is—ah—Ashton?" he inquired of the porter.

"Yes, sah," was the brisk answer.

"Not a—ah—very large place, is it, now?" drawled the passenger.

"Look who's here!" burst out Tom as he hurried forward.

"Why, it's Tubbs—William Philander Tubbs!" ejaculated Sam.

And sure enough, it was Tubbs, the most dudish pupil Putnam Hall had ever known, and one with whom the cadets had had no end of fun.

"My dear old Buttertub, how are you?" called out Tom loudly, and caught the new arrival by the shoulder. "How are you, and how is the wife, and the eight children?"

"Why—ah—is it really Tom Rover!" gasped Tubbs. He stared at Tom and then at Dick and Sam. "What are you—ah—doing here, may I inquire? But please," he added hurriedly, "don't call me Buttertub, and don't say I have a wife and children, when I haven't." And Tubbs looked around to see if anybody had overheard Tom's remark.

"We go to school here," said Dick as he shook hands. "Brill College."

"Well, I never!" gasped the tall dude. "Brill, did you say?"

"That's it," put in Sam.

"I am going there myself."

"You!" roared Tom. "Hail Columbia, happy land! That's the best yet, Tubblets. We'll have dead loads of fun. Did you bring your pet poodle and your fancywork, and those beautiful red and yellow socks you used to wear?"

"I hope you didn't forget that green and pink necktie you used to have," came from Sam, "and the blue handkerchief with the purple variegated border."

"I—ah—I never had those things," stormed Tubbs. "Oh, say, do you really go to Brill?" he questioned, with almost a groan in his voice.

"Sure as you're born," answered Dick. "We'll be glad to have you there, William Philander, You'll be a credit to the institution. We have a few fellows who dress well, but you'll top them all. I know it."

"Do you—ah—really think I can—ah—I will be as well dressed as the—ah—as anybody?" asked the dude eagerly. He was a fair scholar, but his mind was constantly on the subject of what to wear and how to wear it.

"Oh, you'll lead the bunch, and all the girls at Hope will fall dead in love with you," answered Tom

"Hope? What do you mean?"

"That's the seminary for girls. Fine lot of girls there, waiting to see you, Philliam Willander."

"William Philander, please. So there is a girls' school here, eh? That's—ah—very nice. Yes, I like the girls—I always did. But, Tom, please don't call me—ah—Buttertub. I think it's horrid, don't you know."

"All right, Washtub, anything you say stands still," answered Tom cheerfully. "I wouldn't hurt your feelings for a million warts."

"There is the carriage for Brill," said Sam, pointing it out.

"Are you going with me?" asked the dude.

"No. We are not going back until this evening," explained Dick. "We'll see you later."

"Only one other student going with you," ^dded Tom mischievously. "He's kind of queer, but I guess he won't hurt you." He had seen an innocent, quiet youth, named Smith, getting into the college turnout.

"Queer?" asked Tubbs.

"Yes. Gets fits, or something like that. He won't hurt you if you keep your hand to your nose."

"My—ah—my hand to my nose?"

"Yes," went on Tom innocently. "You see, he has an idea that folks are smelling things. So if you keep your hand to your nose he will know you are not smelling anything, so he'll keep quiet."

"I don't—ah—know as I like that," stammered William Philander.

"Carriage for the college!" called the driver, approaching, and before he could say anything the Rovers had Tubbs in the turnout.

"Mr. Smith, Mr. Tubbs," said Dick, introducing the students. Smith bowed, and so did Tubbs. Then the hand of the dude went up to his nose and stayed there.

"Good-by! See you later!" cried Tom.

"Be careful," warned Sam, and tapped his nose.

"I—I think I'd—ah—rather walk," groaned Tubbs.

"It's too far," answered Dick. Then the carriage rolled away. As it passed out of sight they saw William Philander with his hand still tight on his olfactory organ.

"Wonder what Smith will think?" remarked Dick after the three brothers had had a good laugh over the sight.

"He'll certainly think Tubblets queer," answered Sam.

"Tubby will be a barrel of fun," said Tom. "I'm mighty glad he's come. It will aid to brighten up our existence considerably."

The Rover boys were soon on their way to where they were to meet the girls, at a point on the road some distance from Hope Seminary. Soon the whole crowd was in the big touring car, and away they skimmed over a road which, if it was not particularly good, was likewise by no means bad.

"And where are we going?" asked Dora, for that had been kept a secret.

"To a town about twenty miles from here," said Dick. "We are to have supper there, at the hotel."

"How nice!" came in a chorus from the girls.

"I just love automobiling," said Nellie. "I wish I had a car."

"I'll get you one," said Tom, and added in a whisper, "Just wait till we are settled down. We'll have the finest auto rides that——"

"Torn Rover!" cried Nellie, and then blushed and giggled. "Oh, look at the beautiful autumn leaves!" she added, to change the subject. But a second later she gave Tom an arch look that meant a good deal. They seemed to understand each other fully as well as did Dick and Dora.

The ride to Toddville was one long to be remembered. They talked and sang, and the boys told of the meeting with Tubbs and the joke played, and this set the girls almost in hysterics, for they were acquainted with the dude, and knew his peculiarities.

When they arrived at the hotel the spread was almost ready for them, and by the time they had washed and brushed up all felt rather hungry. There was a fine bouquet on the table, and in addition a tiny one at each plate.

"Oh, how nice!" cried Grace.

"Let me pin this on you," said Dora to Dick, and fastened the small bouquet in his buttonhole. The other girls performed a like service for Tom and Sam.

The meal was served in a private dining-room, so all felt free to act as if they were at home. They talked and cracked jokes to their hearts' content, and the boys told their best stories. They also grew serious at times, talking of home and their folks.

"Mamma hasn't heard another word from Tad Sobber," said Dora to Dick.

"And I hope he never appears again," answered the oldest Rover.

The meal was about half finished when one of the waiters came to Dick and said the chauffeur would like to speak to him.

"Very well," answered the oldest Rover, and excusing himself to the others, he went out into the hallway.

"I've just got a telephone message from Raytown," said the chauffeur. "My brother has been hurt at a fire there, and they want me. I don't know what to do. I might send for another man to run the car, but you'll have to wait until he comes. Would you be willing to do that?"

"I might run the car myself," answered Dick. He could see that the chauffeur was much worried over the news he had received.

"Could you do that, sir? If you could it would help me out a whole lot. My brother has a wife and two little children, and she'll be scared to death if Bill is injured."

"Then go right along. Only see to it that the car is in good working order," answered Dick. And then he followed the chauffeur to the shed where the automobile was stored, and had the peculiar working of that make of car explained to him. As my old readers know, Dick had driven a car before, and understood very well how to do it.

As there was no particular need for hurrying, and as it promised to be a fine moonlight night, the Rover boys and their company did not leave the hotel until nearly eight o'clock. Then Dick lit the lamps of the machine and ran it around to the piazza, and the others bundled in.

"Are you sure you can run this car, Dick?" asked Dora a bit timidly.

"Oh, yes, Dora. It is of a make that I have run before, only the other was a five-seat instead of a seven. But this one runs the same way."

"Dick is a born chauffeur," said Sam. "Wait till you see him let the car out to sixty miles an hour."

"Mercy! I don't want to run as fast as that!" cried Grace.

"We'd all be killed if anything should happen," added Nellie.

"Don't you worry. Dick will crawl along at three miles per," drawled Tom. "The moonlight is too fine to run fast. Besides, Dora is going to sit in front with him."

"I'll make the run in about an hour and a half," said Dick, "and that is fast enough. We don't want to get back too early."

"Might go around the block," suggested Sam.

"Around the block would mean about fifteen miles extra," said Dora, who knew all about country "blocks."

"I don't know the roads, so I'll keep to the one we came on," answered Dick. "All ready? Then off we go," he added, and started on low speed, which he soon changed to second and then high. "This is something like!" he cried as he settled back with his hands on the wheel.

"Keep your eyes on the road, and not on Dora," cautioned Tom.

"Say another word and I'll drag you from Nellie and make you run the car," retorted Dick, and then Tom shut up promptly.

Mile after mile was covered, and Dick proved that he could run the big automobile fully as well as the regular driver. The moon was shining brightly, so that it was very pleasant. The party sang songs and enjoyed themselves immensely.

They were still two miles from Ashton when they came to a turn in the road. Here there were a number of trees, and it was much darker than it had been. Dick slowed up a trifle and peered ahead.

Suddenly the front lamps of the machine shone down on something in the roadway that sent back a strange sparkle of light. Dick bent forward and uttered an exclamation of dismay. He turned off the power and jammed on both brakes.

"What's the matter?" cried Sam and Tom in a breath, and the girls gave a scream of fear.

Bang! came a report from under the car.

One of the tires had burst.

AN AUTOMOBILING ADVENTURE

"What did you run over?" asked Sam.

"Look for yourself," returned his big brother. "This is an outrage! I wish I could catch the party responsible for it," he added bitterly.

Dick had stopped the touring car in the midst of a quantity of broken glass bottles. The glass covered the road from side to side, and had evidently been put there on purpose.

"Say, do you think that chauffeur had anything to do with this?" demanded Tom.

"Hardly," answered Dick. "If his story about the fire was not true he'd know he'd be found out."

"Maybe it was done by some country fellow who is running an auto repair shop," suggested Sam. "I've heard of such things being done when business was dull."

"Well, we'll have to fix the tire, that is all there is to it," said the oldest Rover. "Might as well get out while we are doing it," he added to the girls.

"Lucky you stopped when you did," said Tom as he walked around the machine. "If you hadn't we might have had all four tires busted."

"What a contemptible trick to play," said Dora as she alighted.

"Can you mend the tire?" asked Nellie as she, too, got out, followed by her sister.

"Oh, yes, we can mend it—or rather put on another," said Dick. "But we'll examine all the tires first," he added, taking off a lamp for that purpose.

It was found that each tire had some glass in it, and the bits were picked out with care. While this was going on Dick suddenly swung the lamp around so that its rays struck through the trees and bushes lining the roadway.

"Look! look!" he cried. "There is somebody watching us!"

"The fellow who is guilty," added Sam.

"Catch him!" came from Tom, and he made a quick rush forward.

"Say, we've got to get out of here," came in a low voice from among the trees. "Run for all you are worth!"

"I told you to get back," said another voice. "Come on this way."

A crashing through the brushwood back of the trees followed. Dick held up the lamp and threw the rays in the direction of the sounds. He and his brothers caught a glimpse of two boys or men hurrying away.

"Stop, or I'll shoot!" cried Tom, although he had no weapon at his command. But this cry only made the fleeing ones move the faster.

"Sam, you stay with the girls," said Dick quickly. "Tom and I can go after those rascals."

"All right, but take care; they may be dangerous," answered the youngest Rover.

Tom had picked up a good sized stone. Now he hurled it aaead into the bushes. A cry of alarm followed, but whether he hit anybody or not he could not tell.

Holding the lamp so that it would light up the scene ahead, Dick and Tom ran through the grove of trees and then into the thicket of brushwood beyond. They could hear two persons working their way along, and knew they must be the fellows they were after. Once they caught sight of the rascals, but the evildoers lost no time in seeking cover by running for another patch of undergrowth.

"Say, this is fierce!" cried Tom as he stepped into a hole and tumbled headlong.

"Well, it's just as bad for those fellows," answered Dick grimly.

"Yes, but I reckon they are not dressed up as we are." Tom had on his tuxedo and a white tie, and Dick was similarly attired. But over the dress suit each wore a linen coat, buttoned close up to the neck.

The two youths kept on until, much to their surprise, they came out on a back road that was almost as good as the highway they had left. Here was a rail fence, and as they halted at this Tom pointed down the road a distance.

"Somebody on wheels," he cried. "Turn the light on 'em!"

Dick did as requested, and to their astonishment they beheld two young fellows on bicycles. They had their heads bent low over the handlebars, and were streaking along at top speed. Soon a bend of the road hid them from view.

"Those are the chaps who put that glass in the roadway," said Tom.

"I believe you," answered his brother. "They came up here on their wheels and walked through the woods to do it. The question is, who are they?"

"They are enemies of ours," was the prompt answer.

"Yes; but how did they know we were coming this way, and in the auto?"

"They might have overheard us talking to Songbird or Stanley."

"Can they be Flockley and Koswell?"

"More likely Koswell and Larkspur. Flockley hasn't the backbone to do a thing like this. He's too much of a dude."

Dick and Tom took a look around the vicinity. By the light of the lamp they saw where the others had leaped the fence and mounted their bicycles.

"They are the guilty ones, I am sure of that," said Dick. "I wish we had seen their faces."

The youths went back to the auto and told of their adventure. Sam and the girls listened with interest to what they had to say.

"Those boys must be very wicked," said Nellie. "If we had been running fast we might have had a serious accident."

"Shall you accuse them of it?" asked Dora.

"I don't know. I'll think it over," answered Dick.

"The cut-up tire has got to be paid for," said Tom. "Whoever is guilty ought to be made to foot the bill."

While Dick and Sam jacked up the axle of the automobile and put on a new tire—inner tube and shoe combined—Sam set to work and cleaned up the roadway, throwing all the glass into the bushes. Then the new tire was pumped up and tested.

"Now we are all right again," said Dick.

"I am glad we had to mend but one," said Tom. He felt pretty dirty from the job, but he was not going to tell the girls.

All entered the touring car again, and Dick turned on the power. He ran slowly at first to test the new tire.

"All O. K.," he announced presently, and then they went spinning along as before. But the "edge" had been taken off the ride, and they did not seem as free-hearted and full of fun as they had been before the mishap.

It was after ten o'clock when the seminary was reached, and the girls found one of the under teachers waiting for them.

"Young ladies, you were told to be in at ten/* said the teacher severely. "It is now half after."

"We had an accident," answered Dora, and told what it was.

"You must not stay away later than the time originally allowed," said the teacher severely. "Remember that after this, please," and then she dismissed the girls.

When the boys got to the garage where the automobile belonged they told the man in charge about the chauffeur and of what had happened on the road. The garage manager could hardly believe the story about the broken glass.

"You'll have to pay for that tire," he said coldly. "You can't expect to make me stand the loss."

"I suppose not," answered Dick. "You can have the old tire repaired and send the bill to me. And now I want somebody to take us up to Brill just as quickly as it can be done. It is getting late."

"I'll get a man right away," said the manager in a relieved tone, and two minutes later the three Rover boys were being whirled toward the college.

"Do you think those fellows are back yet?" questioned Sam as they sped along the road.

"That's what I want to find out," returned Dick. "That is, provided they came from here."

They left the car at the entrance to the grounds, and the chauffeur at once turned around and started back for Ashton.

"We'll take a look around the gymnasium first," said Dick. "That is where they keep the bicycles and such things."

They hurried in the direction of the gymnasium, and finding the door unlocked, entered. The building was dark and deserted, for it was now after eleven o'clock.

"Hello there!" called a voice from a distance, and a watchman appeared, lantern in hand. "What's wanted?"

"We want to look at the bicycles, Pinkey," answered Dick.

"The bicycles? Ain't goin' for no ride this time o' night, are you?" asked the watchman.

"No. We want to see if any of them have been used."

"Think somebody has been usin' your machine on the sly?"

To this question the Rovers did not reply, for the reason that they had no bicycles at Brill. The watchman led the way to the bicycle room. Here were about twenty bicycles and half a dozen motor cycles, all belonging to various students.

"Ain't half as many as there used to be," remarked Pinkey. "When the craze was on we had about a hundred an' fifty. It's all automobiling now."

The boys looked over the various wheels and felt of the working parts and the lamps. Presently Sam found a hot lamp and Dick located another.

"Who do these machines belong to?" asked Dick.

"There's the list," said the watchman, pointing to a written sheet tacked on the wall. "They are No. 15 and No. 9."

The boys looked at the sheet, and read the names of Walter D. Flood and Andrew W. Crossley, two juniors, whom they knew by sight only.

"They wouldn't play this trick on us," whispered Dick to his brothers. "They must have loaned their bicycles to others."

"Right you are," answered Tom. "We'll have to question them."

"Do you know where they room?"

"No; but we can find out from the register."

They entered their dormitory and found out that Flood and Crossley were in the next building, occupying Room 14 together.

"That's luck," said Sam. "We won't have to wake up anybody else."

It was against the rules to be prowling around the dormitories so late at night, so the Rovers had to be cautious in their movements. They mounted the stairs to the second floor and had to hide in a corner while a proctor marched past and out of hearing. Then, aided by the dim, light that was burning, they located No. 14.

Dick knocked lightly on the door, and receiving no answer, knocked again. Still there was silence.

"Must be pretty heavy sleepers," murmured Tom. "Try the doorknob."

Dick did so, and found the door locked. Then he knocked again, this time louder than before.

"You'll knock a long time to wake them up," said a voice behind them, and turning they saw Frank Holden grinning at them.

"Hello," said Dick softly. "Why, what's wrong?"

"Nobody in that room, that's all," answered the sophomore.

"Don't Flood and Crossley sleep here?" asked Sam.

"Yes, when they are at college, but they got permission to go home yesterday, and they went, and they won't be back until Monday."

At this Dick whistled softly to himself.

"It's all up, so far as finding out who used the wheels is concerned," he said to his brothers. "Whoever took them did so, most likely, without permission."

"I guess you are right," returned Tom.

"Anything I can do for you?" asked Frank Holden pleasantly.

"Nothing, thank you," replied Dick; and then he and his brothers withdrew and made their way to their own rooms as silently as possible. On the way they stopped at the doors of the rooms occupied by Koswell and Larkspur and listened. The students within were snoring.

"No use," said Tom softly. "We'll have to catch them some other way-if they are guilty." And his brothers agreed with him.

CHAPTER XVI

SOMETHING ABOUT A CANE

But if Koswell and Larkspur were guilty, they kept very quiet about it, and the Rover boys were unable to prove anything against them. The bill for the cut-up tire came to Dick, and he paid it.

The college talk was now largely about football, and one day a notice was posted that all candidates for admission on the big eleven should register at the gymnasium.

"I think I'll put my name down," said Tom.

"And I'll do the same," returned Dick, "but I doubt if we'll get much of a show, since they know nothing of our playing qualities here."

There were about thirty candidates, including thirteen who had played on the big team before. But two of these candidates were behind in their studies, and had to be dropped, by order of the faculty.

"That leaves a full eleven anyway of old players," said Sam. "Not much hope for you," he added to his brothers.

"They'll do considerable shifting; every college team does," said Dick; and he was right. After a good deal of scrub work and a general sizing up of the different candidates, four of the old players were dropped, while another went to the substitutes' bench.

It was now a question between nine of the new candidates, and after another tryout Dick was put in as a guard, he having shown an exceptional fitness for filling that position. Tom got on the substitutes' bench, which was something, if not much. Then practice began in earnest, for the college was to play a game against Roxley, another college, on a Saturday, ten days later.

"I hope you win, Dick," said Sam. "And it's a pity you didn't get on the gridiron, Tom," he continued.

"Oh, I'll get on, sooner or later," answered Tom with a grin. "Football is no baby play, and somebody is bound to get hurt."

"You're not wishing that, are you?" asked Songbird.

"No, indeed! But I know how it goes. Haven't I been hurt myself, more than once?"

The football game was to take place at Brill, on the athletic field, and the college students were privileged to invite a certain number of their friends. The Rovers promptly invited Dora, Nellie and Grace, and it was arranged that Sam should see to it that the girls got there.

"Sam will have as good a time as anybody," said Tom. "He'll have the three girls all to himself."

"Well, you can't have everything in this world," replied the youngest Rover with a grin. "I guess football honors will be enough for you this time."

"If we win," put in Dick. "I understand Roxley has a splendid eleven this season. They won out at Stanwell yesterday, 24 to 10."

"I hear they are heavier than we are," said Tom. "At least ten pounds to the man. That is going to count for something."

At that moment William Philander Tubbs came up. He was attired, as usual, in the height of fashion, and sported a light gold-headed cane.

"For gracious sake, look at Tubby!" exclaimed Sam. "Talk about a fashion plate!"

"Hello, Billy boy!" called out Tom. "Going to make a social call on your washerwoman?"

"No. He's going to town to buy a pint of peanuts," said Sam.

"I thought he might be going to a funeral—dressed so soberly," added Dick, and this caused a general laugh, for Tubbs was attired in a light gray suit, patent leathers with spats, and a cream-colored necktie, with gloves to match.

"How do you do?" said William Philander politely, as if he had not seen the others in the classrooms an hour before. "Pleasant day."

"Looks a bit stormy to me," answered Dick, as he saw several sophomores eyeing Tubbs angrily. It was against the rule of Brill for a freshman to carry a cane.

"Stormy, did you say?" repeated the dude in dismay. "Why, I—ah—thought it very fine, don't you know. Perhaps I had better take an—ah—umbrella instead of this cane."

"It would be much safer," returned Dick significantly.

"But I—ah—don't see any clouds," went on William Philander, gazing up into the sky.

"They are coming," cried Tom.

"Stand from under!" called out Sam.

And then the "clouds" did come, although not the kind the dude anticipated. Six sophomores came up behind Tubbs, and while two caught him by the arms a third wrenched the gold-headed cane from his grasp.

"Hi! hi! Stop that, I say!" cried William Philander in alarm. "Let me alone! Give me back my cane!"

"You don't get this cane back, freshie," answered one of the second-year students.

"You must give it to me! Why, Miss Margaret DeVoe Marlow gave me that cane last summer, when we were at Newport. I want——"

"No more cane for you, freshie!" was the cry. And then, to Tubbs' untold horror, one of the sophomores placed the cane across his knee as if to break it in two.

"Don't you break that cane! Don't you dare to do it!" cried the dude, and then he commenced to struggle violently, for the cane was very dear to him, being a birthday gift from one of his warmest lady friends. In the scuffle which followed William Philander had his collar and necktie torn from him and his coat was split up the back.

"Say, this is going too far!" cried Dick, and then he raised his voice: "Freshmen to the rescue!"

"This is none of your affair," growled the sophomore who had led the attack on Tubbs.

"Don't break that cane!" cried Tom. "If you do somebody will get a bloody nose!"

"We'll do as we please!" cried several second-year students.

Then Tom and Sam rushed for the cane and got hold of it. Two sophomores held fast on the other side, and a regular tug-of-war ensued. In the meantime other sophomores were making life miserable for Tubbs. They took his hat and used it for a football, and threw the dude on his back and piled on top of him until he thought his ribs were going to be stove in.

"What's the row?" The call came from Stanley, and he and Max appeared, followed by Songbird and several others.

"Attack on Tubblets!" called Tom. "To the rescue, everybody! Save the cane!"

And then a crowd of at least twelve students surrounded the cane, hauling and twisting it this way and that. It was a determined but good-natured crowd. The sophomores felt they must break the offending stick into bits, while the freshmen considered it the part of honor to save the same bit of wood from destruction.

At last Sam saw his chance, and with a quick movement he leaped directly on the shoulders of one of the second-year students. As the fellow went down he caught hold of two of his chums to save himself. This loosened the hold on the cane, and in a twinkling Sam, aided by Stanley, had it in his possession. He leaped down and started on a run for the dormitory.

"After him! Get the cane!"

"Don't let him get away with it!"

"Nail him, somebody!"

So the cries rang out. Several sophomores tried to head the youngest Rover off, but he was too quick for them. He dodged to the right and the left, and hurled one boy flat. Then he ran around a corner of a building, mounted the steps to a side door, and disappeared from view.

"Hurrah for Sam Rover!"

"Say, that was as good as a run on the football field!"

"That's the time the sophs got left."

"Hi! Where's my cane?" howled William Philander, gazing around in perplexity as soon as the second-year students let go of him.

"Sam has it," answered Tom. "And it wasn't broken, either," he added with pride.

"But—ah—why did he—ah—run away with it?" queried Tubbs innocently.

"To stop the slaughter of the innocents," answered Dick. "He'll give it back to you later. But don't try to carry it again," went on Dick in a low voice.

"Just look at me!" moaned William Philander as he gazed at the wreck of his outfit. "Look at this tie—and it cost me a dollar and seventyfive cents!"

"Be thankful you weren't killed," answered a sophomore. "Don't you know better than to carry a cane."

"I—ah—fancy I'll carry a cane if I wish," answered Tubbs with great dignity.

"Not around Brill," answered several.

"And—ah—why not?"

"Because you're a freshie, that's why. You can wear the colors—because of the necktie rush—but you can't carry a cane."

"Oh—ah—so that's it!" cried William Philander, a light breaking in on him. "But why didn't you come up politely and tell me so, instead of rushing at me like a—ah—like mad bulls? It was very rude, don't you know."

"Next time we'll send you a scented note by special liveried messenger," said one of the second-year students in disgust.

"We'll have it on engraved paper, too," added another.

"Thank you. That will be—ah—better," replied William Philander calmly. "But look at my suit," he continued, and gave a groan. "I can't—ah—make any afternoon calls to-day, and I was going to a pink tea——"

"Wow! A pink tea, boys!" yelled one of the boys. "Wouldn't that rattle your back teeth?"

"Never mind, Tubby. The cook will give you a cup of coffee instead," said Tom.

"I should think you'd feel blue instead of pink," added Spud Jackson.

"Sew up the coat with a shoestring, and let it go at that," suggested Max.

"If you want to paste that collar fast again I've got a bottle of glue," said Songbird.

"Now—ah—don't you poke fun at me!" stormed William Philander. "Haven't I suffered enough already?"

"Why, we're not poking fun; we're weeping," said Tom, and pretended to wipe his eyes with his handkerchief.

"I am so sorry I could eat real doughnuts," said Dick.

"Maybe you want to send a substitute to that pink tea," came from Stanley. "You might call on Professor Sharp."

"Or Pinkey, the watchman," said Max. "He'll do it for a quarter, maybe."

"I—ah—don't want any substitute," growled William Philander. "I—ah—think you are—ah—very rude, all of you. I am going back to my room, that is what I am going to do."

At this Tom began to sing softly:

"Don't be angry, William, darling!
☐ Wipe the raindrops from your eyes.
All your sorrows will be passing
☐ When you're eating Christmas pies!"

"You stop that—you mean thing!" burst out the dude, and then turning, he almost ran for the dormitory, the laughter of the students ringing out loudly after him.

CHAPTER XVII

A MISUNDERSTANDING

"Here's a letter from father—quite an important one, too," said Dick as he joined his brothers in one of the rooms several days later.

"What about?" questioned Sam, while Tom looked up from a book with interest.

"It's about Tad Sobber and that fortune from Treasure Isle," answered Dick.

"What! Has that rascal showed up again?" exclaimed Tom.

"He has; and according to what father says, he is going to make all the trouble possible for the Stanhopes and the Lanings."

"That's too bad," said Sam.

"I'll read the letter," went on Dick, and proceeded to do so. In part the communication ran as follows:

"You wrote that you knew about Sobber's call upon Mrs. Stanhope. Well, after the girls left for Hope Seminary, Sobber and a lawyer named Martin Snodd called upon Mr. Laning and then upon me. Sobber was very bitter, and he wanted to know all about what had been done with the treasure. He claims that he and his uncle, who is dead, were robbed of the boxes. Evidently Sobber and the lawyer had talked the matter over carefully, for the latter intimated that Sobber might settle the case if the Stanhopes and the Lanings would give him seventyfive per cent, of the fortune. Mr. Laning did not wish to go to law, and told Sobber he might be willing to settle for a small amount, say two or three thousand dollars. But Sobber wouldn't listen to this, and went off declaring he would have it all.

"'Since that time Martin Snodd has been busy, and he has obtained a temporary injunction against the Stanhopes and the Lanings, so that they cannot touch a dollar of the money, which, as you know, is now in several banks. The matter will now have to await the result of the case, which will probably be tried in court some months from now.

"'I have learned that Sobber has little or no money, and that Martin Snodd has taken the case on speculation, Sobber to allow him half of whatever he gets out of it. Snodd's reputation is anything but good, so I am afraid he will have a lot of evidence manufactured to order. I have recommended a firm of first-class lawyers to Mrs. Stanhope and the Lanings, and they will, of course, fight the matter to the bitter end."

"This is too bad!" cried Sam after Dick had finished. "So the fortune is tied up so they can't spend a cent of what's left?"

"They can't touch a cent until the courts decide who the fortune really belongs to," answered Dick, "and if Sobber should win, the Stanhopes and the Lanings will have to pay back that which they have already used."

"Oh, how can Sobber win?" cried Tom. "Father said the Stanhope and Laning claims were perfectly legal."

"True, Tom; but you can never tell how a case is going to turn out in court. If this Martin Snodd is a shyster he may have all sorts of evidence cooked up against our friends. Sobber would most likely swear to anything, and so would some of the sailors saved from the *Josephine*. And then there are some of Sid Merrick's other relatives, who would try to benefit by the case. They'd probably testify in favor of Sobber, for they wouldn't expect anything from Mrs. Stanhope or the Lanings."

"But the records of Mr. Stanhope's business deals ought, to be clear," said Sam.

"They are not as clear as one would wish, so father told me," answered Dick. He gave a long sigh. "Too bad! And just when we thought the Stanhopes and the Lanings could sit down and enjoy all that fortune."

"I wonder if the girls know of this yet?" mused Tom.

"Most likely they have had word from home," answered Dick.

"It will make them feel pretty sore," said Sam.

"Yes, it would make anybody feel sore," answered the oldest Rover. "We'll have to drive over and see, the first chance we get."

When they met the girls the boys learned that they knew all about the affair. All were worried, and showed it.

"This will upset mamma very much," said Dora. "I am afraid it will put her in bed."

"It's too bad, but it can't be helped," said Dick.

"Dick, do you think we ought to buy Sobber off?"

"No. He doesn't deserve a cent of that money."

"Papa says the case will not come up for a long time, the courts are so crowded with cases," remarked Nellie. "He is about as worried as anybody, for he has already spent several thousand dollars, and if we lose he won't know how to pay it back."

"We'll lend him the cash," said Tom promptly, and for this Nellie gave him a grateful look.

The boys did their best to cheer up the girls, but their efforts were not entirely successful. All felt that the coming legal contest would be a bitter one, and that Tad Sobber and the shyster lawyer who was aiding him would do all in their power to get possession of the fortune found on Treasure Isle.

The girls were coming to the football game with Sam, and all said they trusted Brill would win the contest.

"We are all going to carry Brill flags," said Grace, "and I am going to root—isn't that what you call it?—as hard as I can."

"Then we'll be sure to win!" cried Dick.

Yet the oldest Rover was by no means confident. The Brill eleven had heard that their opponents were in the pink of condition. They had played three games already, and won all of them. Brill had played against the scrub only, which was hardly a test of what it could do.

The day for the contest dawned clear and bright, and early in the afternoon the visitors from Roxley, Hope, and other institutions of learning, as well as from Ashton and other towns, commenced to pour in. They came on foot, in carriages and automobiles, and on bicycles, and soon the grandstand and the bleachers were filled to overflowing. Flags and college colors were in evidence everywhere, and so were horns and rattles.

While Dick was waiting to catch sight of the carriage containing Sam and the girls from Hope he saw another turnout approaching. In it were Mr. Sanderson and his daughter Minnie.

"Why, how do you do, Mr. Rover!" cried the girl pleasantly.

"Very well," answered Dick politely, raising his cap. "And how are you?"

"Oh, fine! I made papa drive me over to see the game. It's going to be something grand, so I've heard," went on Minnie, and then she added: "Thought you and your brothers were coming to see us?"

"We—er—we haven't had much time," stammered Dick. He did not care to add that when he went to see a young lady it was always Dora Stanhope, and that Tom and Sam called only on Nellie and Grace Laning.

"I've been expecting you," said the girl with a pretty pout.

"Have Dudd Flockley and Jerry Koswell been there since?"

"Yes, both of them came once, and Flockley came after that, but I refused to see them. Mr. Flockley wished to bring me to see this game, but I sent word that I was going with papa."

"He ought to know enough to stay away by this time," said Dick. He could think of no other remark to make.

"Can I get a seat anywhere?" asked Minnie, looking anxiously over in the direction of the grandstand. ' "I think so. Wait, I'll look."

"Hold on," put in Mr. Sanderson. "Just you take Minnie along, Mr. Rover. I'll go and take care of the hoss. I can stand anywhere and look on."

Minnie prepared to spring to the ground, and there was nothing to do but for Dick to assist her. He wondered if Sam was coming with Dora and the others, but did not see them. Then he led the way through the crowd to where some seats were reserved.

"I think you'll be able to see nicely from here," he said.

"Oh, I know I shall." She smiled broadly at him. "You are very kind. I don't know what I should have done if I had been alone—there is such a jam. Oh, I do hope you win!" And Minnie beamed on Dick in a manner that made him blush, for he saw that several were watching them.

"I must go now. It is getting late," said Dick after a little more talk. He turned, to see Sam, Dora and the Laning girls only a few seats away. Dora was looking fully at Minnie Sanderson with wide open eyes and a flush mounting to her cheeks.

"Oh, so you've arrived!" cried Dick cheerily, but his voice had a catch in it. Somehow he felt guilty, he could not tell why.

"Yes, here we are," answered Nellie.

"And what a crowd!" added Grace. Dora said not a word. She had stopped looking at Minnie and her eyes were directed to nothing at all on the football field.

— "Well, Dora, are you going to wish me success?" asked Dick, bound to say something.

"Oh, I guess all your lady friends will wish you that," was the answer in a voice that did not seem like Dora's at all.

"Why, what's the matter?" he asked in a low voice meant only for her ears.

"Nothing."

"But there is, Dora."

"You had better go down to the field now. I see the other players are getting ready."

"But if you are angry at me——"

"Oh, I am not angry, so please leave me alone!" And now Dora turned still further away, while something like tears began to spring into her eyes.

Dick drew back, for her tone of voice nettled him. He felt he had done nothing wrong. He did not see that look in her eyes, or he would have understood how much she was hurt. He turned, nodded pleasantly to Nellie and Grace, and hurried from the grandstand.

"Where have you been?" asked Tom when he appeared in the dressing-room.

"Up on the stand, talking to the girls," was Dick's short answer.

"Anything wrong? You look out of sorts."

"No, nothing is wrong," answered the oldest Rover. But he felt that there was something trery much wrong, yet he could not tell Tom.

"I didn't do anything out of the way, I'm sure I didn't," Dick murmured to himself as he prepared to go out on the gridiron. "Any gentleman would have found a seat for Miss Sanderson. I suppose Dora saw me talking to her, and now she imagines all sorts of things. It isn't fair. Well, I don't care." And Dick whistled to himself, just to keep up his courage. He did care a great deal.

At last he was ready, and he followed Tom out on the field. The Roxley team had just come out, and their friends were giving them a royal welcome.

"Roxley! Roxley!" they shouted. "They are the boys to win!"

"It's Brill this time!" was the answering rally, and then horns and rattles added to the din, while banners were waved gaily in the bracing autumn air.

Dick looked toward the grandstand, trying to single out Dora. Instead, his eyes met those of Minnie Sanderson, and she waved both her banner and her handkerchief. He answered the salute, and then turned to look where Dora and the Lanings were sitting. Nellie and Grace, as well as Sam, cheered him, but Dora took no notice. But she waved her flag at Tom.

This last action made Dick's heart sink, figuratively speaking, to his shoes. How could a fellow hope to play and win with his girl cutting him like that? But then of a sudden he shut his teeth hard.

"I'll win even if she doesn't care," he told himself. "I'll not do it for her, or myself—I'll do it for the honor of Brill!"

CHAPTER XVIII

THE GREAT FOOTBALL GAME

It is not my intention to give all the particulars of that game of football between Brill and Roxley, for the reason that I have many other things to tell about. Yet I feel that I must tell something of that great second half, which nobody who saw it will ever forget.

In the first half Roxley had the kick-off, and they played such a fierce whirlwind game that before the leather had been on the gridiron eight minutes they scored a touchdown. Then they made another touchdown, and just before thfc whistle blew for the end of the first half one of their players kicked a goal from the field.

And Brill scored nothing.

More than this, the playing was so rough that two of the Brill eleven and one from Roxley had to retire from the field.

Of course the visitors went wild with joy, and shouted themselves hoarse. They waved their colors, swung their rattles, and tooted their horns for fully five minutes, while the silence among the Brill contingent was so thick it could be "cut with a knife," as Sam afterward expressed it.

"It's all over," murmured Stanley with a glum look on his face. "Their eleven this year are too heavy for us."

"We can't meet them in mass play, that's certain," was Dick's comment. "If we are going to gain anything at all it must be by open work."

"Tom Rover can take Felton's place," came the order from the head of the team, and Tom at once threw off the blanket he had been using and got into practice with another new man and some others.

Dick felt sore, physically and mentally. He had been roughly used by two of the Roxley players, and had made a fumble at a critical moment. And all during that heartrending first half Dora had not noticed him at all!

The coach did some plain talking to the players while in the dressing-room, and told them of where he thought Roxley might be weak—at the left end.

"Don't mass unless you absolutely have to," were his words of caution. "They have the weight, but I don't think they have the wind. Keep them on the jump. I think that is your only chance."

When the whistle blew for the second half the Brill eleven came out on the gridiron with a "do or die" look on their faces.

"Now pile it into 'em!" cried the coach. "Don't give 'em time to think about it!"

Whether it was this caution, or the very desperateness of the case, it would be hard to say, but true it is that Brill went at their opponents "hammer and tongs" from the very start. They avoided all wedge work and confined themselves as much as possible to open playing. More than this, they used a little trick Dick had once played when on the eleven at Putnam Hall. The ball was passed from right to left, then to center, and then to left again, and then carried around the end for a gain of twenty-five yards. Then it was picked up again, turned back and to the left once more, and forced around the end for twenty yards more.

"That's the way to do it!" yelled several of the Brill supporters.

"Over with it, while you've got the chance!"

The ball was forced back by sheer weight of Roxley, but only for five yards. Then the Brill quarter-back got it, sent it over to Tom, and in

"RUN, DICK! RUN RUN!"—*Page* 189.

The Rover Boys at College.

a twinkling Tom "nursed" it to where he wanted it and kicked a goal from the field.

"Hurrah! hurrah! hurrah!"

"That's the way to do it!"

"Now, then, for another!"

"By the great Julius Cæsar!" cried Sam. "Isn't that fine?"

"Oh, it was grand!" exclaimed Nellie, and she waved her banner directly at Tom, and he waved his hand in return. Just then Nellie felt as if she could go and hug him.

"It certainly was fine," said Grace, "but it's only one goal, and they have such a big score," she pouted.

"Never mind. We won't be whitewashed, anyway."

"It's a pity they didn't have Tom in the first half," said Dora. Although her heart was strangely sore, she nevertheless felt proud of what Tom had accomplished.

Again the two elevens went at it, and now Roxley tried again to force the center by a rush. But to their surprise Brill shifted to the left—that one weak spot—and got the ball on a fumble by the Roxley half-back. There was more quick action by four of the Brill players, and when the scrimmage came to an end the leather was found just three yards from the Roxley goal line.

And then came that awful struggle, where muscle met muscle in a strain that was truly terrific. Roxley was heavier, but its wind was going fast. Brill held at first, then went ahead—an inch—a foot—a yard.

"Hold 'em! Hold 'em!" was the Roxley cry. But it was not to be. The yard became two, and then the leather went over with a rush.

"A touchdown! A touchdown for Brill!"

"Now make it a goal!" was the cry, and a goal it became, the Brill quarter-back doing the kicking.

From that moment on the battle waged with a fury seldom seen on any gridiron. Brill, from almost certain defeat, commenced to scent a victory, and went into the play regardless of physical consequences. Tom had his thumb wrenched and Dick had his ankle skinned, but neither gave heed to the hurts. Indeed, they never noticed them until the game was at an end.

And then came Dick's hour of triumph. How he got the ball from the burly Roxley right guard nobody could exactly tell afterward, but get the ball he did, and rounded two rival players before they knew what was up. Then down the field he sped, with his enemies yelling like demons behind him, and his friends on the benches encouraging him to go on. He saw nothing and heard nothing until on the grandstand he perceived a slender girlish form arise, wave a banner, and fairly scream:

"Dick! Dick! Run! run! run!"

"It's Dora," he thought. "Dora sees me! She wants me to win!"

It was the last bit of inspiration he needed, and as a Roxley full-back came thundering up to him he threw the fellow headlong. Then straight as an arrow from a bow he rushed for the goal line, crossed it, and sank limply down in front of the grandstand.

"Hurrah for Dick Rover!"

"Say, wasn't that a dandy run?"

"Those brothers can certainly play!"

"It's Brill's game now! Roxley is going to pieces!"

Amid a great din the leather was taken down into the field and the goal was kicked.

"Want to get out of the game?" Dick was asked as he came down, breathing heavily.

"No, not unless I'm put out," was the gritty answer.

"You'll not be put out. That was the finest run ever made on this field."

What had been said about Roxley going to pieces was, in part, true. Several shifts were made in the players, but this did not aid the eleven. With twelve minutes more to play, Brill kept up its winning streak, and secured another touchdown and goal and then a safety. When the whistle finally blew the ball was well in Roxley's territory.

"Brill wins!"

"Say, wasn't that a great game? All Roxley the first half and all Brill the second."

"Talk about a team pulling itself together! I never saw anything like what Brill did in the second half."

"Nor I."

"Those two Rover boys are wonders."

So the talk ran on. Of course, Roxley was keenly disappointed, but it tried not to show it, and sang songs and cheered its opponents. And Brill cheered the enemy, as is the custom.

Tom and Dick were surrounded by a host of friends, and had to shake hands over and over again, and had to have their hurts washed and bound up. Both wanted to get to where Sam and the girls had been left, but this was impossible for quite a while, and then, much to their surprise, they found their brother and the others had gone, and Minnie Sanderson had departed also.

"Wonder where they went to?" questioned Tom. "I told Sam we'd be along as soon as possible."

To this Dick did not answer. He was thinking deeply. Was Dora still angry, in spite of how she had cheered him?

"There they are!" cried Tom a few minutes later, as he and Dick walked toward the river. He had seen Nellie and Grace on a bench in the sun, surrounded by a number of other visitors. He hurried up to them, his brother following more slowly. "Where are Dora and Sam?" he questioned, looking around.

"Dora asked to go back to the seminary," answered Nellie, and looked sharply at Dick.

"To the seminary?" repeated Tom in wonder.

"Why, how's that?"

"She said she had a—headache."

"Is that so? That's too bad! Why didn't she wait for Dick to take her over?"

"I—I don't know, Tom." Nellie lowered her voice, so Dick might not hear. "Something is wrong between them. I don't know what it is."

"Wrong? Why, how can that be? I didn't hear of anything," Tom now spoke in a whisper.

"Well, I am sure something is wrong. They acted queer when Dick came to the grandstand before the game commenced. Dora's heart was not in the game at all. She was ready to go before it was over."

"By the way, Tom, who was that other girl?" asked Grace pointedly.

"What other girl?"

"The girl Dick was talking to here on the grandstand."

"Oh, that was the farmer's daughter we helped when we first came to Ashton. Her name is Minnie Sanderson. We told you about her."

"She seems to think a good deal of Dick," was Nellie's comment.

"Why, you don't mean——" Tom looked around, expecting to see Dick close by. "Hello! Where did he go?" he cried.

"Dick is walking back to the college," said Grace.

"Hi, Dick!" called out Tom to his brother. "Where are you going?"

"Up to my room," answered Dick.

"Yes, but see here——"

"Can't see now. I'll see you later," answered Dick. He waved his cap and bowed.

"Goodby, Nellie! Good-by, Grace!" And then he turned on his heel and continued on his way to the dormitory building.

"Well, if this doesn't beat the Chinese!" murmured Tom.

"He must be very angry over something," murmured Nellie.

"I think he might have come and shook hands when he said good-by," said Grace with a pout.

"I think so myself," answered Tom. "Say, do you think it's that girl?" he went on, in his usual blunt fashion.

"It must be," answered Nellie, who was equally frank on all occasions. "I don't know what else it could be."

"But Dick hasn't done anything. I am sure of it. Why, I don't think he has seen her since we stopped at her home that time."

"Well, he seemed very attentive to her here in the stand," said Grace, "and if you'll remember, he didn't meet us when we arrived. I am sure Dora looked for him."

Tom gave a long sigh and shrugged his shoulders.

"This takes the edge off the victory," he murmured. "I thought the six of us would have a jolly time for the rest of the day."

"It certainly is too bad," answered Nellie. "But I don't think Dora is to blame."

"Oh, of course a girl will stick up for another girl," retorted Tom, bound to say something in his brother's defense.

"Tom Rover!" cried Nellie, and then she showed that she was displeased.

It was quite a while before Sam came back from seeing Dora to the seminary. He, too, thought Dora was more to blame than Dick, and this did not altogether please Grace. As a consequence there was a coldness all around, and the rest of the afternoon dragged most woefully. Dick did not return, and at last Sam and Tom saw the Laning girls back to their school.

"A pretty mess of fish!" muttered Sam on returning to Brill.

"Yes; and where is it going to end?" asked Tom dolefully. It was the first time there had been such cold feelings all around.

CHAPTER XIX

MORE COMPLICATIONS

The football eleven celebrated the victory that evening by bonfires and by something of a feast. Of course Tom and Dick were present, as were also Sam and a host of others, but it must be confessed that the Rovers did not enjoy themselves.

"See here, Dick," said Tom after the festivities were over, "what is this trouble between you and Dora?"

"Don't ask me, ask her," returned Dick shortly. "She knows more about it than I do."

"She won't say a word," came from Sam. "She said she didn't feel well, that's all; and I know that wasn't true altogether."

"Was it that Minnie Sanderson?" went on Tom.

"If it was, it wasn't my fault," answered Dick.

"But what did you do?" insisted Tom. He was bound to get at the bottom of the affair.

Thereupon Dick was compelled to relate all that had happened, which, in truth, was not much.

"And is that all?" asked Sam.

"Yes."

"I don't see why she should be put out over that," said Tom slowly. "But then girls are queer. The more you know them the less you understand them."

"Grace and Nellie take Dora's part," said Sam with a deep sigh. "It has put us all somewhat on the outs."

"I am sorry to hear that," answered Dick, and his tone of voice showed that he was sincere. "But I don't know what I can do," he added helplessly. "I don't want to be on the outs with anybody, but if Dora is bound to turn the cold shoulder to me——" He did not finish.

Following the game with Roxley, Brill played two other games with a college from Delton and another from Speer. The game with the latter college resulted in a tie, but Delton was beaten by Brill by a score of 16 to 10. Tom and Dick played in both games, and won considerable credit for their work.

During these days the boys did not see the girls, nor did they hear from them. Thanksgiving was passed at Brill, only a few of the students going home. Among the number to leave were Dudd Flockley and" Jerry Koswell, and they did not return until a week later.

The dude and his crony, as well as Larkspur, were still down upon the Rovers, but for the present they kept quiet, the reason being that they were behind in their lessons and had to work hard to make up. But all were watching their chances to do the Rover boys some injury on the quiet.

Dick, Tom and Sam got along well in their studies. The only trouble they had in the classroom was with Professor Sharp, who made them "toe the mark" upon every occasion. But they took good care to obey the rules, so the irascible teacher got no chance to lecture or punish them.

The boys got a number of letters from home, and these brought news that the law case Tad Sobber had instituted against the Stanhopes and the Lanings was being pushed vigorously. Mr. Rover wrote that he felt certain the shyster lawyer Sobber had on the case was going to present a great mass of "evidence," no doubt manufactured for the occasion.

"It's a shame!" cried Tom after hearing this. "Such a lawyer ought to be in prison!"

"The thing of it is to prove he is doing something wrong," answered Dick. "It is one thing to know the truth and quite another to prove it in court."

"If the case should be lost the Lanings will be poorer than ever," said Sam.

"That is true, Sam. I wish we could do something, but I am afraid we can't."

Fate seemed bound to make matters worse for the Rover boys. On a clear, cold Saturday afternoon in December the three brothers and Songbird went out to look for nuts in the woods near Ashton. They had heard that the seminary girls occasionally visited the woods for that purpose, and each was secretly hoping to run across Dora and the Lanings.

It did not take the boys long to reach the woods, and they soon found a spot where hickory nuts were plentiful. They had brought some bags along, and were soon hard at work gathering the nuts.

While thus occupied they heard a number of girls coming along. At first they fancied the newcomers might be from the seminary, but soon saw that they were natives of the place. They were five in number, and among them was Minnie Sanderson.

"Why, how do you do?" said Minnie, coming up with a smile on her face. "How strange to meet out here!" And then she shook hands with each of the Rovers, and speedily introduced her friends, and the Rovers introduced Songbird.

Minnie was neatly attired in a brown dress, with a brown hat to match, and while she did not look anyway "stunning," she made an attractive appearance. Her friends, too, were pretty, and well dressed, and all were very jolly.

"It's a nice bunch, all right," murmured Tom to Sam. "I like their open-hearted way of talking."

"So do I," answered the youngest Rover.

The girls joined the boys in gathering nuts, and so spent an enjoyable hour roaming through the woods. Often the Rovers and Songbird would knock down the nuts with sticks and stones and leave the girls to gather what they wanted.

"We like to have a large quantity of nuts on hand for the winter," said Minnie to Dick. "Then, when there is a deep snow on the ground we can sit before the blazing fire and crack nuts and eat them. You must come over some time this winter and help," she added.

"Perhaps I will," murmured Dick. He had to admit to himself that Minnie was very cordial and that she was by no means bad looking. He did not wonder why Flockley and Koswell were so anxious to call upon her.

Roaming through the woods caused Songbird to become poetic, and while they rested in the sunshine, and picked some of the nuts that Tom and Sam had cracked, he recited some verses composed on the spur of the moment:

"Hark to the silence all around!
The well-trained ear doth hear no sound
The birds are silent in their nest,
All tired Nature is at rest.
The brook in silence finds its way
From shadows deep to perfect day.

The wind is dead, there is no breeze———"

"To make a fellow cough and sneeze!"

murmured Tom, and gave a loud ker-chew! that set all the girls to laughing.

"That isn't right!" declared Songbird half angrily. "There is no sneeze in this poem."

"Oh, excuse me. I only thought I'd help you out," answered Tom soberly. And then the would-be poet continued:

"The wind is dead, there is no breeze
To stir the bushes or the trees.
Full well I know, as here I stand,
That Solitude commands the land!"

"Good! Fine! Immense! Great!" cried Sam enthusiastically. "Hurrah for Solitude!"

"Why, Mr. Powell, you are a real poet," said one of the girls gravely. And this pleased Songbird greatly.

"You'll have to write in my autograph album," said another, and the would-be poet readily consented. Later he inscribed a poem in the book three pages long.

At last it came time to leave the woods, and the boys walked with the girls toward the road. As they did this they heard the sound of wheels.

"Must be a carriage coming," said Dick, and stepped into the roadway to see, followed by the others in the party. A few seconds later a turnout rumbled into sight. It was the Hope Seminary carryall, and it contained half a dozen girls, including Dora, Nellie and Grace.

"Hello! Look there!" cried Tom, and raised his cap, and the other boys did the same. Dora and her cousins looked at the crowd, and their faces flushed. They bowed rather stiffly, and then the carryall bowled on its way.

"Why, those are your friends!" cried Minnie, turning to the Rovers. "Don't you want to speak to them?"

"It's too late now," answered Dick. He had a curious sinking sensation in his heart that he could not explain. He looked at his brothers, and saw that they, too, were out of sorts.

The passing of the carryall put a damper on matters, and the girls felt it. They talked with the Rovers and Songbird a few minutes longer and then turned in one direction while the Brill students turned in another.

"Fine lot of girls," was Songbird's comment. "Very nice, indeed. And they know how to appreciate poetry, too," he added with satisfaction.

"Oh, yes, they are all right," answered Dick carelessly. Somehow, he was now sorry he had gone to the woods after nuts.

"I am going to call on all of them some time," went on Songbird. "That Minnie Sanderson told me she plays the piano, and sings. I am going to get her to sing a new song. I am writing. It goes like this———"

"Excuse me, Songbird; not now," said Dick. "I want to do an extra lesson." And he hurried off, while Sam and Tom did the same.

Two hours later Dick ran into William Philander Tubbs, who had been down to town in company with Stanley.

"Had a lovely time, don't you know," drawled William Philander. "While Stanley posted some letters and addressed some picture postals I did up the shops. And what do you think? I found a beautiful new maroon necktie, and it was only a dollar—same kind they would charge one seventy-five for in the big cities. And I saw a new style of collar, and some patent-leather pumps that have bows with loose ends, and——"

"Some other time, Billy," interrupted Dick. "I'm in a hurry now."

"Oh, I'm sorry. But, Dick, one other thing. I met Miss Stanhope and her cousins."

"You did?" And now Dick was willing to listen. "Where?"

"At one of the stores. They were doing some buying, in company with those chaps you don't like."

"The chaps I don't like! You don't mean——" Dick paused in wonder.

"I mean that Flockley chap and his chums, Koswell and Larkspur."

"Were Miss Stanhope and the Misses Laning with those fellows?" demanded the elder Rover.

"They seemed to be. They were buying fruit and candy, and I think Flockley treated to hot chocolate. The girls seemed glad enough to see me, but I—ah—didn't want to—ah—break in, you know, so I came away."

"Where did they go after having the chocolate and candy?"

"I don't know. I didn't see them after that." And there the talk came to an end, for several other students appeared. Dick walked off in a thoughtful mood.

"Deeper and deeper!" he told himself, with something like a groan. Then he hunted up Sam and Tom.

"Going with Flockley and that crowd!" cried Tom. "Not much! I won't have it!" And he commenced to pace the floor.

"What are you going "to do about it?" asked Sam.

"Call on the girls and talk it over—and you and Dick are going with me."

"I'll not go," declared Dick.

"Neither will I," added Sam.

"Yes, you shall—and to-night," said Tom firmly.

CHAPTER XX

DAYS OF WAITING

Eight o'clock that evening saw the three Rovers on their way to Hope Seminary. Tom was the leader, and it had taken a good half hour's arguing on his part to get Dick and Sam to accompany him.

"You'll make a fool of yourself, and make fools of us, too," was the way Sam expressed himself.

"Most likely they won't want to see us," was Dick's opinion.

"If they don't want to see us, really and truly, I want to know it," answered Tom bluntly. "I don't believe in this dodging around the bush. There is no sense in it." It had angered him to think Nellie had been seen in the company of Flockley and his cronies, and he was for "having it out" without delay.

"Well, you'll have to lead the way," said Dick. "I'm not going to make a call and have Dora send down word that she can't see me."

"She won't do that," said Tom. "I know her too well."

"Well, you call on Nellie first."

"I'm not afraid," retorted Tom. He was so "worked up" he was willing to do almost anything.

The nearer the three students got to the seminary the slower they walked. Even Tom began to realize that he had undertaken what might prove a very delicate mission.

"I think it would have been better to have sent a letter," suggested Sam. "Let's go back and write it before we go to bed."

"And put down something in black and white that you'd be sorry for afterward," grumbled Dick.

At the entrance to the seminary grounds they halted again, but then Tom caught each brother by the arm and marched them up to the front door and rang the bell.

A maid answered their summons and led them to a reception-room. A minute later one of the teachers appeared.

"Why, I thought you young gentlemen knew the young ladies had gone away," said the teacher after they had mentioned the object of their visit. "They said they were going to send you a note."

"Gone away!" echoed Dick.

"Yes. The three left for home on the late afternoon train. Mrs. Stanhope and Mrs. Laning said it was a matter of business. Then you didn't get their note?"

"We did not," answered Tom.

"That is too bad. I am sure they spoke of sending it. Wait, I will ask Parks, our messenger, about it."

The teacher left the room, and the Rover boys looked speculatively at each other.

"They must have been getting ready to leave when Tubbs saw them," said Dick.

"And we never knew they were going," added Sam bitterly.

"The matter of business must refer to that Sobber case," said Tom. "I don't know what else could take them home."

"Maybe they have lost the case and must give the treasure up," said Sam. "In that case, Mr. Laning would have to take the girls away from such an expensive place as this."

In a few minutes the lady teacher came back.

"Parks says he took three notes, addressed to Richard, Thomas and Samuel Rover. He says he went over to Brill this morning with them and gave them to a man named Filbury."

"Filbury, eh?" said Dick, naming an old man who worked around the dormitories. "Well, we didn't get them, and I am very sorry."

"So am I, Mr. Rover," said the teacher.

"Do you know how long the young ladies will be gone?"

"They could not tell. They said they would send letters after they arrived home."

This was all the seminary teacher could tell, and a minute later the Rovers said good night and left. All hurried from the grounds in deep thought.

"We must find Filbury and see what he did with those letters," said Tom, and his brothers agreed with him.

When they reached Brill they located the man they were after fixing a light in one of the halls.

"Where are those letters you got for us this morning, Filbury?" asked Dick sternly.

"Letters?" asked the old man, who was rather absent minded. "I don't remember no letters, Mr. Rover."

"I mean the three letters which Parks of Hope Seminar) 7 ' gave you for me and my brothers."

"Oh, them. I remember now. Let me see. Yes, I got them, and one for Mr. Flockley, too. I gave him all the letters. He said he'd hand 'em to you." And apparently satisfied, Filbury resumed his work on the light.

"When was this?" demanded Sam.

"About eleven o'clock. I hope it's all right. I would have delivered the letters myself, only I had a lot of work to do."

"It is not all right, and we are going to look into the matter at once," said Dick, and hurried off with Tom and Sam at his heels. They went straight to the room occupied by Flockley and Koswell, and knocked on the door. There was a stir within, a few whispered words, and then the door was opened.

"What do you want?" asked Jerry Koswell. Flockley was sitting by the table, reading.

"Flockley, what did you do with those letters you got from Filbury for us?" demanded Dick, striding into the room.

"Letters?" asked the dude carelessly. "Oh, I put them on the table in Tom and Sam's room."

"When?"

"This morning."

"They weren't there after dinner," said Sam.

"Nor after supper, either," added Tom.

"Look here, do you accuse me of stealing your letters?" demanded Flockley, rising as if in anger.

"No; but we want to know where they are," answered Tom.

"I told you what I did with them. I wouldn't have touched the letters, only Filbury asked me to do the favor. If they are not on the table maybe the wind swept them to the floor. Did you look?"

"No."

"Then you had better."

"You might have spoken about them, Flockley," said Dick coldly. "Any other student would have done so."

"Or you could have handed us the letters at lunch," added Sam.

"I am not your hired man!" cried Dudd Flockley. "Next time I'll not touch the letters at all!" And then he dropped back into his chair and pretended to read again.

"If we don't find the letters you'll hear from us again," said Dick. And then he and his brothers retired.

They entered the room occupied by Sam and Tom and lit up. The notes were not on the table.

"Here they are!" cried Sam, and picked them up from the floor, under the edge of Tom's bed. They looked rather mussed up, and all of the Rovers wondered if Flockley had opened and read them.

"I don't think he'd be any too good to do it," muttered Tom as he opened the note addressed to himself.

It was from Nellie, and rather cool in tone. It said all were called home on account of the case at court, but did not give any particulars. At the bottom was mentioned the time of departure from Hope and also from Ashton. The notes from Dora and Grace contained about the same information, and Grace added that she wanted Sam to write to her.

"If we had had these letters this afternoon we might have gone to Hope instead of nutting," said Tom bitterly.

"They must have expected to see us, either there or at the depot," said Sam. "Otherwise they wouldn't have been so particular about mentioning the time of departure from both places."

"Yes, I guess they expected to see us, or hear from us," said Dick, and breathed a deep sigh.

"Well, they did see us—when we were with Miss Sanderson and her friends."

"What must they have thought—if they imagined we had received the letters?" groaned Tom.

"They thought we cut 'em dead," replied Sam. "Isn't this the worst ever? And all on Flockley's account! I'd like to punch his nose!"

"I'd like to be sure of one thing," said Dick, a hard tone stealing into his voice. "Did Flockley just happen to be in Ashton when the girls got there, or did he open and read these letters and then go on purpose, with Koswell and Larkspur?"

"Say, that's something to think about!" cried Tom. "If he opened the letters I'd like to make him confess."

"Well, one thing is certain," said Dick after the matter had been talked over for a while, "we missed a splendid chance to talk matters over with the girls. It is too bad!" And his face showed his concern.

"And you didn't even want to go to Hope with me," commented Tom, with a humor he could not repress.

"Wish we had gone yesterday," answered Sam bluntly. He could read "between the lines" of the note he had received, and knew that Grace wanted to see him just as much as he wanted to see her.

Sam said he was going to write a letter that night, and finally Tom and Dick agreed to do the same.

"But I shan't write much," said Dick. "I am not going to put my foot in it." Nevertheless he wrote a letter of four pages, and then added a postscript of two pages more. And the communications Sam and Tom penned were equally long.

"We'll not trust 'em to the college mail," said Tom. "We can take 'em to the post-office when we go to church to-morrow." And this was done.

After the letters were posted the brothers waited anxiously for replies, and in the meantime buckled down once more to their studies. It was now well along in December, and one morning they awoke to find the ground covered with snow.

"Snowballing to-day!" said Tom with a touch of cheerfulness, and he was right. That day, after class hours, the students snowballed each other with a will. The freshmen and the sophomores had a regular pitched battle, which lasted the best part of an hour. All of the Rovers took part in the contest, and it served to make them more cheerful than they had been for some time.

"What's the good of moping?" said Tom. "We are bound to hear from the girls sooner or later." Yet, as day after day went by, and no letters came, he felt as downcast as did his brothers.

The boys were to go home for the Christmas holidays, and under ordinary circumstances they would have felt gay over the prospect. But now it was different.

"Going to send Dora a Christmas present?" asked Tom of Dick, a few days before the close of the term.

"I don't know. Are you going to send anything to Nellie?"

"Yes, if you send something to Dora."

"Sam says he is going to send Grace a writing outfit and a book of postage stamps," went on Dick.

"That's what they all need," growled Tom. "It's a shame! They might at least have acknowledged our letters."

The boys did not know what to do. Supposing they sent presents to the girls, and got them back? They held a meeting in Dick's room and asked Songbird's advice.

"Send them the nicest things you can buy," said the would-be poet. "I am going to send a young lady a gift—a beautiful autograph album, with a new poem of mine, sixteen verses in length. It's on 'The Clasp of a Friendly Hand.' I got the inspiration once when I—er—But never mind that. It's a dandy poem."

"Who is the album to go to?" asked Tom indifferently.

"Why—er—Minnie Sanderson," answered Songbird innocently. "You see, we. have gotten to be very good friends lately."

CHAPTER XXI

HOME FOR THE HOLIDAYS

The next day the Rover boys went down to Ashton to see what they could find in the stores. Dick said he wanted to get something nice for his Aunt Martha, Tom wanted something for his father, and Sam said he thought Uncle Randolph was deserving of a gift that was worth while.

Yet when they got into the largest store of which the town boasted all seemed to gravitate naturally to where the pretty things for the ladies were displayed.

"There's a dandy fan," murmured Tom. "Nellie likes fans very much."

"So does Grace," returned Sam. "Say, what are you going to do?"

"What are you going to do, Sam?"

"I'm going to get one of those fans and send it, along with a box of bonbons and chocolates," answered the youngest Rover boldly. "And I'm going to send Mrs. Laning a pair of kid gloves," he added.

"Then I'll send a fan, too," answered Tom, "and I'll send Mrs. Laning a workbox. I know she'd like one."

In the meantime Dick was looking at some fancy belt buckles and hatpins. He knew Dora liked such things.

"I'll just take Songbird's advice and get the best I can and send them," he told himself. And he picked out the best buckle he could find, and likewise a handsome hatpin, and had them put into a fancy box, along with a fancy Christmas card, on which he wrote his name. Then he purchased a five-pound box of candy at the confectioner's shop, and Tom and Sam did the same.

This was the start, and now that the ice was broken, and the first plunge taken, the boys walked around from one store to another, picking up various articles, not alone for the folks at home, but also for their various friends. And they added a number of other things for the girls, too.

"It's no worse to send four things than two," was the way Tom expressed himself.

"Right you are," answered Dick. Now that they had decided to send the things they all felt better for it.

On the day school closed there was another fall of snow, and the boys were afraid they would be snowbound. But the train came in, although rather late, and all piled on board.

At Oak Run, their railroad station, they found Jack Ness, the Rover's hired man, awaiting them with the big sleigh. Into this they tumbled, stowing their dress-suit cases in the rear, and then, with a crack of the whip, they were off over Swift River, and through Dexter's Corners, on their way to Valley Brook farm.

"And how are the folks, Jack?" asked Sam as they drove along, the sleighbells jingling merrily in the frosty air.

"Fine, Master Sam, fine," was the hired man's answer.

"And how have you been?"

"Me? Oh, I've been takin' it easy—since Master Tom quit plaguing me."

"Why, I never plague anybody," murmured Tom, with a look of injured innocence on his round face. He reached out and caught some snow from a nearby bush. "Say, Jack, what is, that on the horse's hind foot?" he went on.

"Where? I don't see nuthin'," answered the hired man, and leaned over the dashboard of the turnout to get a better view. As his head went forward Tom quickly let the snow in his hand fall down the man's neck, inside his collar.

"Hi! hi! Wow!" spluttered Jack Ness, straightening up and twisting his shoulders.

"Say, what did you put that snow down my back for?"

"Just to keep you from sweating too much, Jack," answered Tom with a grin.

"At your old iricks again," groaned the hired man. "Now, I reckon the house will be turned upside down till you go back to college."

When the boys got in sight of the big farm house they set up a ringing shout that quickty brought their father and their uncle and aunt to the door. And behind these appeared the ebony face of Aleck Pop, the colored man who was now a fixture of the Rover household.

"Hello, everybody!" cried Tom, making a flying leap from the sleigh the instant it drew up to the piazza. "Isn't this jolly, though?" And he rushed to his Aunt Martha and gave her a hug and kiss, and then shook hands with his father and his Uncle Randolph. Dick and Sam were close behind him, and went through a similar performance.

"My! my! Don't squeeze the breath out of me!" cried Mrs. Rover, as she beamed with delight. "You boys are regular bears!"

"Glad you got through," said their father. "It looks like a heavy storm."

"It does my heart good to see you again," said Uncle Randolph. "I trust you have profited by your stay at Brill." He was well educated himself, and thought knowledge the greatest thing in the world.

"Oh, we did profit, Uncle Randolph," answered Tom with mischief showing in his eyes. "Dick and I helped to win the greatest football game you ever heard about."

"Tom Rover!" remonstrated his aunt, while Aleck Pop doubled up with mirth and disappeared behind a convenient door.

"We brought home good reports," said Sam. "Dick stands second in the class and Tom stands fifth. That's not so bad in a class of twenty-two."

"And Sam stands third," put in Tom.

"That is splendid!" said Anderson Rover. "I am proud of you!"

"And so am I proud," added Randolph Rover.

"You'll all be great men some time," said their Aunt Martha. "But come into the sitting-room and take off your things. Supper will be ready in a little while. But if you want a doughnut beforehand——"

"Hurrah for Aunt Martha's doughnuts!" cried Sam. "I was thinking of them while riding in the train."

"Well, you shall have all you wish during the holidays," answered his aunt fondly.

They were soon settled down and relating the particulars of some of the things that had happened at Brill. None of the boys cared to tell of the coldness that had sprung up between themselves and the girls. They simply said they knew the girls had gone home.

"That was an outrage," said Mr. Rover with considerable warmth.

"An outrage?" repeated Dick doubtfully. "What do you mean?"

"Perhaps you didn't hear the report that was circulated at Hope Seminary concerning them."

"We heard no report, excepting that they had been called home."

"Somebody circulated a story that they were going to school on money that did not belong to them—that their folks had confiscated a fortune belonging to others. Grace wrote to her mother that the story was being whispered about everywhere, and it was making them all miserable; and that's the main reason for their going home."

"What a contemptible thing to do!" cried Tom. "Who do you suppose is guilty—Tad Sobber?"

"I can think of nobody else. He is so angry he would do anything to injure them and us."

"And what of the case?" asked Sam. "Will it coma up in court soon?"

"Some time next Spring."

"And what do the lawyers think of our side winning?' questioned Dick eagerly.

"They say it depends largely upon the evidence the other side submits. It is possible that the case may drag on for years."

"What a shame!" murmured Dick.

It continued to snow all that night and the next day, and Christmas found the family all but snowbound at Valley Brook.

"Merry Christmas!" was the cry, early in the morning, and the boys tumbled out of bed and dressed in a hurry. Then they went below, to find a stack of presents awaiting them. They quickly distributed the gifts they had brought and then looked at their own. They had almost everything their hearts could desire.

Yet each youth felt a pang of disappointment, for among all the gifts there were none for them from the Stanhopes or the Lanings.

"We are out of it," said Dick laconically to his brothers.

"So it appears," answered Tom soberly. For once, all the fun was knocked out of him.

"Well, I am glad I didn't forget them, anyway," said Sam bravely. But he wondered how it was Grace could treat him so shabbily.

The boys passed the day as best they could in reading and playing games, and in snowballing each other and Jack Ness and Aleck Pop.

"My! my! But dis am lik old times at Putnam Hall!" said the colored man, grinning from ear to ear when Tom hit him on the head with a snowball. "Hab yo' fun while yo' am young, Massa Tom."

"That's my motto, Aleck," answered Tom. "Have another." And he landed a snowball on the colored man's shoulder.

"I move we go down to the post-office for mail," said Dick toward evening. "We don't know what we may be missing."

"Second the motion!" cried Tom. "The post-office it is, if we can get through."

"Can't no hoss git through these drifts," came from Jack Ness.

"We'll hitch up our biggest team and take our time," said Dick. "We have got to get down to the post-office somehow." He was hoping desperately that he would find a letter from Dora there.

When the old folks heard of it they shook their heads doubtfully. But the boys pleaded so strongly that at last they were allowed to go. They got out a strong cutter and the best pair of horses on the farm, and bundled up well.

"If you can't make it, drive in at one of the neighbors," said Mr. Rover on parting.

"We will," answered Dick.

CHAPTER XXII

WORD AT LAST

It was a long, hard drive to Dexter's Corners, and by the time the boys arrived there they were chilled through and through and the team was pretty well winded. They went directly to the postmaster's house, for the office was in a room of the building.

"I'll see if there are any letters," said the postmaster, and went off. He returned with a picture postal for Mrs. Randolph Rover and two advertising circulars for her husband. There were also a newspaper and a magazine for the boys' father.

"And is that all?" asked Dick, his heart sinking.

"That's all."

"Not worth coming for," muttered Tom as they turned away.

"The mail didn't come in this morning," shouted the postmaster after them. "You'll have to wait for more stuff until the train arrives at Oak Run."

"Let us go over to the Run and see if we can learn anything about the trains," said Sam, a spark of hope springing up in his breast.

They drove over the river, and as they did so they heard the whistle of a locomotive.

"Something is coming," cried Dick.

"Perhaps it's only the night freight," returned Tom.

When they reached the depot the train was standing there. It was the morning accommodation, nine hours late. They saw some mail bags thrown off and also several express boxes and packages.

Curiosity prompted Dick to inspect the express goods. He uttered a cry of joy.

"A box for us!" he exclaimed. "And from Cedarville!"

"Where?" cried Tom and Sam, and ran forward to look the box over. It was two feet long and a foot high, and equally deep, and was addressed to R., T. and S. Rover.

"From the girls, I'll bet a snowball!" cried Tom joyfully. "Hurry up and sign for it and we'll see what it contains."

The agent was at hand, for he was the ticket agent and station master as well, and they soon signed for the box. Then they took it to a secluded corner of the station, and with a borrowed hammer and chisel pried off the cover.

The sight that met their gaze filled them with pleasure. There were several packages for each of the boys, from the girls and from Mrs. Stanhope and Mrs. Laning. There were some beautiful neckties, some books, and some diaries for the new year, and a box of fudge made by the girls. Dora had written on the flyleaf of one of the books, wishing Dick a Merry Christmas and a Happy New Year, and similar sentiments from Nellie and Grace appeared in the books for Tom and Sam.

"Say, I reckon this was worth coming for," remarked Sam.

"Rather," answered Dick.

"Wouldn't have missed it for a million dollars," added Tom.

"Maybe the mail bag has some letters for us," went on Sam. He was disappointed that no note had accompanied the gifts.

"We'll take the bags to the office and see," said Dick, and this was done a little later, after the box had been closed and put in the cutter and carefully covered with a robe. In the bags were found letters from their old friends, Hans Mueller and Fred Garrison, and a postal from Dave Kearney, but that was all.

"Well, we mustn't expect too much," said Dick. "Remember, we didn't send any letters."

"But we will now, thanking them for all these nice things," said Sam quickly.

It was nearly midnight before the boys got home again, and their folks were much alarmed about them. They were almost exhausted, but very happy, and they showed their new presents with great pride.

"They are dear girls!" said Mrs. Rover. "It was splendid of them to remember you this way, and splendid of Mrs. Stanhope and Mrs. Laning, too."

The next morning was spent in writing letters. It was rather hard at first to say just what they wanted to, but after they had started the letters grew and grew, until each was ten pages or more. They told about meeting Minnie Sanderson and the other girls by accident, and about not getting the notes until that night, and Dick added the following to his letter to Dora:

"And now let me tell you something in secret. Songbird Powell has developed a very, very strong liking for Miss Sanderson, the girl Tom and Sam and I aided when first we came to Brill. He talks about her a good deal, and took her to a concert at Ashton one evening. He said he was going to give her an autograph album for Christmas and write in it an original poem sixteen verses long, on 'The Clasp of a Friendly Hand.' That is pushing matters some, isn't it? We all wish him luck."

"There, that ought to make her understand how I feel about Miss Sanderson," said Dick to himself. And then he ended the letter by stating he hoped they would meet again soon so that they could have a good long talk.

On the day after the letters were mailed the storm cleared away and the sun came out brightly. The boys went for a long sleigh ride, and visited some friends living in that vicinity. Then they helped to clear off a pond, and on New Year's day went skating.

"And now back to the grind," said Tom with a little sigh.

"Never mind. Remember summer will soon be here," answered Sam. "And then we can go on a dandy trip somewhere."

The next day found them back at Brill. This was Saturday, and the school sessions were resumed on Monday. They went at their studies with a will, resolved to get marks that would be "worth while" at the June examinations. They were asked to join the college basketball team, but declined, and took regular gymnasium exercise instead. Much to their surprise, Dudd Flockley was put on the team.

"I don't think that dude will make good," said Tom, and he was right. Flockley made some bad errors during the first game played, and was lectured so severely that he left the team in disgust, and Songbird Powell was put in his place. Then the team won three games straight, which pleased all the students of Brill greatly. Minnie Sanderson was at two of the games, and she applauded Songbird heartily. The two were certainly warm friends. Dick spoke to Minnie, but did not keep himself long in her company.

At last, after waiting much longer than they had expected, the boys received letters from

Dora and the Lanings. The girls had been on a visit to some relatives in Philadelphia, and had just received the letters mailed from Oak Run.

The three Rovers read those letters with deep interest. They told about what the girls had been doing, and related the particulars of the trouble at Hope Seminary. It was all Tad Sobber's work, they said, and added that Sobber had written that he would not only get the treasure, but also disgrace them all he possibly could.

"The rascal!" muttered Dick when he read this. "He ought to be put in prison!"

Dora's letter to Dick was an especially tender epistle, and he read it several times in secret. He was glad that the misunderstanding between them was being cleared away. He wished she might be near, so that he could go and see her.

"I'd take a run to Cedarville if it wasn't so far," he told his brothers.

"I'd go along," answered Tom, and Sam said the same.

"Perhaps we can run up there during the spring vacation," went on Dick.

There was little more snow that winter, but the weather remained bitterly cold until well into February. The boys had considerable fun snowballing, and skating on the river. Racing on skates was a favorite amusement, and Sam and Tom won in a number of contests.

One day Tom was skating by himself. He was doing some fancy figures, and he did not notice the approach of Jerry Koswell, who was skating with a young lady from Ashton. Tom came around in a circle, and Jerry, who was looking at the young lady instead of where he was going, bumped into Tom. Both of the students went down, Tom on top.

"Hi! What do you mean by this?" burst out Koswell in a rage.

"What do you mean?" retorted Tom, getting up.

"You knocked me down on purpose!" howled Jerry.

"It was as much your fault as mine."

"It wasn't my fault at all. I've a good mind to punch your face!" And having gotten to hit feet, Koswell doubled up his fists threateningly.

At this the young lady let out a scream.

"Oh, please don't fight!" she cried. And then she skated to a distance and disappeared in a crowd.

"You keep your distance, Koswell," said Tom coldly. "If you don't- ——"

He got no further, for just then Koswell let out with his right fist. The blow landed on Tom's shoulder and sent him spinning away a distance of several feet.

CHAPTER XXIII

THE SPRINGTIME OF LIFE

"A fight! a fight!" came from the crowd, and soon Tom and Koswell were surrounded by a number of students and some outsiders.

The blow from the bully angered Tom greatly, and skating forward he made a pass at Koswell. But the latter ducked, and then came back at Tom with a blow that sent the funloving Rover into several students standing by.

"Say, Rover, look out, or Jerry Koswell will eat you up!" said one of the seniors.

"Koswell is a good scrapper," came from another.

"I gave him one lesson and I can give him another," answered Tom. "There, take that!"

He turned swiftly and rushed at Koswell. One blow after another was delivered with telling accuracy, and Koswell went flat on his back on the ice. When he got up his nose was bleeding.

"I'll fix you!" he roared. "Come on to shore and take off your skates!"

"I'm willing," answered Tom recklessly. He knew fighting was against the rules of the college, but he was not going to cry quits.

The pair moved toward the shore, the crowd still surrounding them. They soon had their skates off.

"Now, Jerry, do him up brown!" came from Larkspur, who was present.

"Give him the thrashing of his life!" added Flockley, who had come up.

"He has got to spell able first, and he doesn't know the alphabet well enough to do it!" answered Tom.

"What's up?" cried a voice from the rear of the crowd, and Dick appeared, followed by Sam.

"Koswell attacked me, and wants to fight, and I am going to accommodate him," said Tom.

"Don't you butt in!" growled Koswell.

"I won't," answered Dick. "But I want to see fair play." He knew it would be useless to attempt to get Tom to give up the fight.

Without preliminaries the two faced each other, and Kosweli made a savage rush at Tom, aiming a blow for his face. Tom ducked, and landed on his opponent's chest. Then Koswell hit Tom on the arm and Tom came back at him with one on the chin. Then they clinched, went down, and rolled over and over.

"Stop, you rascal!" cried Tom suddenly. "Can't you fight fair?"

"What's up?" asked Dick, leaping forward.

"He bit me in the wrist!"

"I—I didn't do anything of the kind!" howled Jerry Koswell.

"Break away, both of you!" ordered Dick. "We'll see into this."

Tom let go, but Koswell continued to hold fast. Seeing this, Dick forced the two apart and both scrambled up.

"See here, this isn't your fight!" said Larkspur to Dick.

"It will be yours if you don't shut up!" answered Dick, so sharply that Larkspur shrunk back in alarm.

"I didn't bite him!" grumbled Koswell.

"He did—right here!" answered Tom positively. "Look!"

He pulled up his sleeve and showed his wrist. There in the flesh were the indentations of a set of teeth.

"You coward!" said Sam. "You ought to be drummed out of Brill!"

"That's worse than using a sandbag," added Dick.

"I—I didn't do it," muttered Koswell. He looked around as if he wanted to slink out of sight.

"You did!" cried Tom. "And take that for it!" And before the brute of a youth could ward off the blow he received Tom's fist in his right eye. Then he got one in the other eye and another in the nose that made the blood spurt freely. He tried to defend himself, but Tom was "fighting mad," and his blows came so rapidly that Koswell was knocked around like a tenpin and sent bumping, first into Flockley, then into Larkspur, and then into some bushes, where he lay, panting for breath.

"Now have you had enough?" demanded Tom, while the crowd marveled at his quickness and staying powers.

"I—I——" stammered Koswell.

"If you've had enough, say so," went on Tim. "If not, I'll give you some more."

"I—I'm sick," murmured Koswell. "I was sick this morning when I got up. I'll—I'll finish this with you some other day."

"All right, Koswell," answered Tom coolly. "But when you go at it again, do it fairly, or you'll get the worst of it. Remember that!"

"Hurrah for Tom Rover!" was the cry from Stanley, and the cheer was taken up on all sides. Jerry Koswell sneaked away as soon as he couhi,, and Flockley and Larkspur followed him.

"He'll have it in for you, Tom," said Sam as he and his brothers got away from the crowd. "Most likely he is mad enough to do anything."

"Oh, he was mad before," declared Tom. "I am not afraid of him."

Everybody thought there might be another fight in the near future, but day after day went by and Koswell made no move, nor did he even notice Tom. He kept with Flockley and Larkspur, and the three were often noticed consulting together.

At last winter was over, and the warm breath of Spring filled the air. Much to the pleasure of the boys, they got news that Dora, Nellie and Grace were going to return to Hope, regardless of the reports that had been circulated about them.

"Good! That's what I call pluck!" cried Dick.

They learned when the girls would arrive at Ashton, and got permission to go to town to meet them. It must be confessed that all of them were a trifle nervous, in spite of the warm letters that had been sent.

When the train came in they rushed for the parlor car, and then what a handshaking and greeting followed all around! Everybody was talking at once, and after the first minute or two there was nothing but smiles and laughter.

"I am so sorry that—you know," whispered Dick to Dora.

"So am I," she answered. "What geese we are, aren't we?"

"Well, we won't have any more misunderstandings, will we?" he went on, squeezing her hand.

"Never!" she declared, and gave him an arch look. "And you say Songbird is—is——"

"Going with Miss Sanderson? Yes; and they are as thick as two peas. But, Dora, I never was—er—very friendly with her. I—I——"

"But you—you talked to her at that football game, Dick. And you didn't meet me when Sam——"

"I know. But I had to find her a seat, after she about asked me to. I wanted to be with you, I did really, dear."

"Who said you could call me dear?" And now her eyes were as bright as stars.

"I said so, and I'm going to—when we are alone. The future Mrs. Dick Rover deserves it," he went on boldly, but in a very low voice.

"Oh, Dick, you're awful!" cried Dora, and blushed. But somehow she appeared mightily pleased.

The boys drove the girls to the seminary, and by the time the boarding-school was reached all were on the best of terms once more.

"Mamma wanted us to come back," explained Dora. "She says, even if we do lose that fortuneshe wants me to have a better education, and she will pay the bill for Nellie and Grace, too."

"It will make the Lanings quite poor, I am afraid, if the fortune is lost," replied Dick gravely.

"I know it, Dick, but we'll have to take what comes."

"Have you heard from Sobber or his lawyer lately?"

"Nothing since he threatened to disgrace us."

"You must watch out for him. If he attempts to bother you while you are here let us know at once."

"We will."

"I hope the case in court is decided soon, and in your favor."

"Say, stop!" cried Tom, as they were turning into the gate at the seminary.

"What's up?" asked Sam, while Dick halted the team he was driving.

"Here comes a buggy along the side road. Just look who is in it!"

All turned to look in the direction of the turnout which was approaching. As it came closer the Rover boys recognized it as one belonging to Mr. Sanderson. On the front seat sat Songbird, driving, with Minnie Sanderson beside him. On the rear seat was William Philander Tubbs, in company with one of Minnie's friends—a girl the Rovers had met while nutting.

"There's a happy crowd!" cried Tom after they had passed and bowed and smiled.

"No happier than we are," said Dick as he looked meaningly at Dora.

"You are right, Dick," she answered very earnestly.

AT THE HAUNTED HOUSE

"Boys, I've got a proposition to make," said Dick, one Friday afternoon, as he and his brothers, with Songbird and Stanley, were strolling along the river bank.

"All right. We'll accept it for twenty-five cents on the dollar," returned Tom gaily.

"What is it, Dick?" asked Songbird.

"Do you remember the haunted house at Rushville, the place Mr. Sanderson called the Jamison home?" asked Dick of his brothers.

"Sure!" returned Sam and Tom promptly.

"Well, I propose we visit that house to-morrow and investigate the ghosts if there are any."

"Just the thing!" cried Sam.

"I've heard of that place," said Stanley. "I am willing to go if the rest are."

"If I go as far as Rushville I might as well go on to the Sanderson home," said Songbird, "who could not get Minnie out of his mind.

"Well, we'll leave you off—after we have interviewed the ghosts," answered Dick with a laugh.

"Do you believe in ghosts?" asked Stanley with a faint smile.

"No. Do you?"

"Hardly, although I have heard some queer stories. My aunt used to think she had seen ghosts."

"She was mistaken," said Tom. "There are no real ghosts."

"Say, Tom, how could a ghost be real and still be a ghost?" asked Songbird, and this question brought forth a general laugh.

The boys sat down on a bench in the warm sunshine to discuss the proposed visit to the deserted Jamison place, and it was arranged that they should drive to the spot in a two-seated carriage. Then, while the Rovers and Stanley investigated to their hearts' content, Songbird was to drive on to the Sanderson home for a brief visit.

"But, mind, you are not to stay too long," said Dick. "An hour is the limit."

"I'll make it an hour by the watch," answered the would-be poet. "Say, I just thought of something," he went on, and murmured softly:

"To-morrow, ere the hour is late,
We shall go forth to investigate.
The Jamison ghost
Shall be our host;
We trust we'll meet a kindly fate!"

"That's as cheerful as a funeral dirge!" cried Tom.

"We don't want to meet any kind of a fate," added Sam. "We want to have some fun."

While the boys were discussing the proposed trip to Rushville they did not notice that Larkspur was close at hand, taking in much that was said. Presently Larkspur sauntered off and hunted up Jerry Koswell.

"The Rovers are going off to-morrow," he said. "Where do you suppose they are going?"

"I am not good at guessing riddles," answered Koswell rather sourly. He hated to hear the Rover name mentioned, since it made him think of his defeat at Tom's hands.

"They are going to the old Jamison place at Rushville."

"Well, what of it?"

"I was thinking," answered Larkspur meaningly. "You said you would like to square up with the Rovers, and with Tom especially."

"So I would. Show me how it can be done and I'll go at it in jig time." And now Koswell was all attention.

"I happen to know that Tom Rover and Professor Sharp are on the outs again," said Larkspur. "The professor wouldn't like anything better than to catch him doing something against the rules."

"Well, what do you propose, anyway?" demanded Jerry Koswell.

"Come up to the room and I'll tell you," answered Larkspur, and then the two hurried off and, joined by Dudd Flockley, hatched out a scheme to get the Rovers into dire trouble with the college authorities. They had a number of preparations to make, and paid a hurried visit to Ashton and several other places, Flockley hiring a runabout for that purpose.

Saturday proved clear and warm, and the Rovers and their friends started directly after lunch for Rushville in a two-seated carriage, hired from a liveryman of Ashton. As they did not wish to excite any curiosity, they told Tubbs and Max that they were going out merely for a long ride.

"Going to call on Miss Stanhope and the Misses Laning, I suppose," said William Philander.

"No. They have some lessons to make up today," answered Dick, and this was true; otherwise the Rovers might not have been so willing to spend their time at the haunted house.

No sooner had the Rovers and their two friends driven away from Brill than an automobile dashed up on the side road, and Flockley, Koswell and Larkspur climbed in. The automobile kept to the side road until the Rovers turnout was passed, then took to the main highway, passing the upper end of Ashton.

"Here is where you can leave us," said Koswell to the chauffeur. "I'll see to it that the machine comes back safely."

"You are sure about being able to run it?" asked the man.

"Of course. I ran a big six-cylinder at home."

"Very well, then. This is a fine car, and there would be trouble with the boss if anything happened to it."

"Nothing is going to happen, so don't worry," answered Koswell coolly. Then the chauffeur left, and the automobile dashed on its way in the direction of Rushville.

As the Rovers and their chums were out purely for pleasure, they took their time in driving to Rushville, going there by way of Hope Seminary. They thought they might catch sight of Dora and the Lanings, but were disappointed.

"Too bad that they have got to grind away on such a fine day as this," said Dick.

"Well, such is life," returned Sam. "One good thing, schooldays won't last forever."

"Just wait till the summer vacation comes!" cried Tom. "I'm going to have the best time anybody ever heard about."

"What doing?" questioned Stanley.

"Oh, I don't know yet."

They took their time climbing the long hill leading to the haunted house, and it was just three o'clock when they came in sight of the dilapidated structure, almost hidden in the tangle of trees and underbrush.

"Now, Songbird, you've got to be back here by four, or half after, at the latest," said Dick as he and his brothers and Stanley got out. "No spooning with Minnie till six."

"Huh! I don't spoon," grumbled the wouldbe poet. "I am—er—only going to show her some new verses I wrote. They are entitled——"

"Keep them for Minnie!" cried Sam. "And remember what Dick said. We are not going to hang around here after dark."

"Scared already?" asked Songbird.

"No, but enough of this place is enough, that's all."

"I'll be back, don't worry," said Songbird, and, away he drove at a swift gait, leaving the Rovers and Stanley in the roadway in front of the house said to be haunted.

It was certainly a lonely spot, no other house being in sight, for Rushville lay under the brow of a hill. The boys stood still and listened. Not a sound broke the stillness that surrounded the deserted house.

"It sure is a ghostlike place," remarked Stanley. "I shouldn't care to come here at midnight."

"Oh, that wouldn't make any difference, if you had a light," answered Dick. The thought of a ghost had never bothered him very much.

Boldly the four boys entered what had once been a fine garden. The pathway was now overrun with weeds and bushes, and they had to pick their way with care. Then they ascended the piazza, the flooring of which was much decayed.

"Look out that you don't fall through somewhere, and break a leg," cautioned Tom. "This is worse than it looks from the outside."

"Wait till we get inside," said Sam. "Glad we brought a lantern." For a light had been taken along at the last minute.

They pushed open the front door and entered the broad hall. As they did so they heard a noise at the rear of the place.

"What was that?" asked Stanley nervously.

"Sounded like a door closing," answered Dick.

"Hello!" called out Tom. "Is any one here?"

To this call there was no answer. Nor was the noise they had heard repeated.

"Come on," said Dick bravely. "I am going to walk right through the house, room by room, from top to bottom."

"And we'll all go along," said Tom and Sam.

"Well, I am with you," came from Stanley. But he plainly showed that he did not relish what was before him.

CHAPTER XXV

IN THE HANDS OF THE ENEMY

The first room the boys entered was the parlor. It was totally dark, the blinds of the windows being tightly closed. It was full of cobwebs, which brushed their cheeks as they passed along.

"Certainly this was a fine mansion in its day," said Dick, as he threw the rays of the lantern around. "But it is utterly worthless now," he added as he gazed at the fallen ceilings and rotted woodwork.

"I fancy the ghosts are nothing but rats and bats," said Tom. "Come on," he continued. "It's damp enough to give one the rheumatism."

From the parlor they passed to a sitting-room. Here there was a huge open fireplace, filled with ashes and cobwebs. As they entered the room they heard a rushing noise in the chimney.

"What's that?" cried Stanley anxiously.

"Birds," answered Dick. "I suppose they have made their home in the chimney, since it is not used for fires."

In a corner of the sitting-room was an old table, and on it several musty books. The boys looked the books over, but found little to interest them. As relics the volumes were of no value.

"Come on to the dining-room," said Tom.

"Maybe we'll find something good to eat."

"Ugh! I don't want anything here," answered Stanley with a shudder.

"Wouldn't you like a piece of ghost pie, or some specter doughnuts?" went on Tom, who was bound to have his fun.

"Nothing, thank you, Tom."

The dining-room of the house was in a wing, and to get to it they had to pass through a pair of folding doors which were all but closed. As they did so all heard a peculiar rustling sound, but from whence it came they could not tell.

"What was that?" asked Sam.

"I don't know," answered his oldest brother.

"Say, this room looks as if it had been used lately," cried Tom, as the rays of the lantern illuminated the apartment. "Why, it's quite homelike!"

"Maybe some tramps have had their headquarters here," said Dick. "It would be just like them to single out a spot like this."

"Yes, provided they weren't afraid of ghosts," came from Stanley.

"Tramps aren't usually afraid of anything but work," answered Tom dryly. "But this is queer, isn't it?" he added, as he picked up an empty cigar box. "Somebody must smoke good cigars—these were imported."

"Here is an empty liquor flask," said Stanley.

"And here are some empty wine bottles," added Sam.

"And here are some decks of playing-cards," put in Dick. "Yes, some persons have certainly used this as a hangout."

"What is this in the fireplace?" asked Tom as he pointed to something smoking there.

"It certainly has a vile smell!" exclaimed Stanley, making a wry face.

"That shows somebody has been here recently," was Dick's comment. "We had better be on guard if they are tramps."

"I can't stand that smell," said Tom. "I am going to get out."

The stuff in the fireplace, whatever it was, now burned up more brightly. It gave off a peculiar vapor that made the boys dizzy.

Tom turned to a door that led to the kitchen of the house. The door was shut, and he tried in vain to open it. The others were behind him, and they, too, tried to open the barrier.

"Must be locked from the other side," said Tom. "Come on out the way we came in. Gracious! Isn't that awful stuff that is burning?" he added, for the vapor now filled the room completely.

In sudden alarm the four boys turned back toward the folding doors through which they had entered the dining-room. To their consternation, the doors were tightly shut.

"Who shut these?" asked Dick as he tried to open one of the doors.

"I didn't," said Sam.

"Neither did I," added Tom.

"Nobody touched the doors!" ejaculated Stanley. "It must be some of the ghost's work."

"Nonsense!" answered Dick sharply. "Somebody shut the doors—and locked 'em," he added after trying both. "Hi, you!" he called. "Open these doors, and be quick about it!"

"Thou fool, to come here!" exclaimed a hollow voice from the other side of the doors.

"It's the ghost! I said it was!" said Stanley.

"It's somebody fooling us," answered Tom. "Open the door, or we'll smash it down!" he added in a loud voice.

Instead of a reply there came a weird groan and then the rattle of some heavy chains. Stanley turned pale and began to tremble, but the Rovers were not much impressed.

"We don't believe in ghosts, so you might as well let us out!" cried Dick. "That stuff you set on fire is smothering us!"

At this there was a murmur from the next room, but what was said the prisoners did not know.

"Come on, let us get out of a window!" cried Tom. His head was commencing to swim, and he could hardly see.

"Tha—that's it," murmured Sam. "Say, I'm—I'm—going——" He did not finish, but sank to the floor in a heap.

"Sam has been overcome!" cried Dick in horror.

"Oh, if only we hadn't come here!" groaned Stanley. "I—the window—I—am—smothering!" He took another step forward and then fell. Dick tried to pick him up, but went down also, with his brain in a whirl and strange lights flashing before his closed eyes.

Tom was the last to be overcome. He reached a window, only to find it tightly locked. He smashed the glass, but could not open the blinds. Then he went down; but before he closed his eyes he saw the door to the kitchen open and several masked faces appeared. He tried to say something, but the words would not come, and then all became a terrible dark blank around him.

For about half a minute after Tom went down nothing was done. Then the door to the kitchen was thrown wide open and four figures appeared. All wore sheets and masks.

"You are sure it won't kill any of them, Parwick?" asked a voice that sounded like Jerry Koswell's, and which was far from steady.

"Yes, I'm sure," answered the voice of a stranger. "But we don't want to leave them in this room too long. Take 'em below."

"If we get found out——" said another, and one could readily recognize Flockley's voice.

"We won't get found out," put in a fourth person. It was Larkspur. "Come ahead, and don't waste time here."

With great haste the masked ones picked up the three Rovers and Stanley and dragged them into the kitchen of the old house. Then one after another the unconscious ones were taken down into a dark and musty cellar and placed on some straw.

"Now to fix up the evidence!" cried Koswell. "We must be quick, or it may be too late!"

For all of a quarter of an hour the three Rover boys and Stanley Browne lay where they had been placed on the moldy straw. They breathed with difficulty, for the strange vapor still exercised its influence on their lungs.

At last Sam stirred and opened his eyes.

"Wha—what's the matter with me?" he murmured, and then sat up.

He could see next to nothing, for the cellar was dark. His head ached keenly, and he could not collect his senses. He also felt somewhat sick at the stomach.

"Dick! Tom!' he called. "Where are you?"

There was no reply, but presently he heard somebody stir.

"Don't—don't kill me!" murmured Stanley. "Take the ghosts away!"

"Stanley!" called Sam. "Whe—where are we?"

"Who—who is tha—that?" stammered Stanley, sitting up.

"It is I—Sam!"

"Whe—where are we, Sam?"

"I—I don't know."

"My head is go—going around like—like a top."

"So is mine. Tom! Dick!"

"Is that you, Sam?" came faintly from the elder Rover as he opened his eyes.

"Yes. Where is Tom?"

"Here, I guess, beside me." Dick shook his brother. "Tom! Tom! Wake up!" he cried. But Tom continued to lay quiet with his eyes tightly closed.

Sam was feeling in his pocket for a matchbox, and presently he brought the article forth and made a light. He was still so dizzy he could scarcely see about him. Stanley had fallen back again, gasping for breath.

By the dim light afforded by the match the two brothers looked at Tom. He was gasping in a strange, unnatural fashion.

"I believe he is choking to death!" said Dick hoarsely. "Air! He must have air!" He arose unsteadily to his feet. "Bring him here!"

And he made for a closed cellar window with all the strength he could command.

THE EVIDENCE AGAINST THEM

Fortunately a loose brick lay handy and with this Dick smashed out the panes of glass in the cellar window. Another window was opposite, and this he likewise demolished. At once a current of pure air swept through the place.

"Hold him up to the window," said Dick as he staggered around. And he and Sam raised Tom up as best they could.

"If we could only get outside," mumbled Sam. His head was aching worse than ever.

"I'll see what I can do," answered his oldest brother, and stumbled up the narrow stairs. To his joy, the door above leading to the kitchen of the house was unfastened.

Not without great labor did the two brothers carry Tom to the floor above. Then they went after Stanley, who was conscious, but too weak to walk. As they stumbled around they sent several empty liquor bottles spinning across the floor, and one was smashed into pieces.

"I wish I knew how to revive him," said Dick as he and Sam placed Tom near the open doorway. "Wonder if there is any water handy?"

"Oh, my poor head!" came from Stanley. "I feel as if I had been drinking for a month!"

"Wonder what it was?" murmured Sam. "I—I can't make it out at all."

"Nor I," added Dick. "But come, we must do what we can for Tom." And he commenced to loosen his unconscious brother's tie and collar.

Suddenly a form darkened the outer doorway of the kitchen, and to the surprise of the boys Professor Abner Sharp showed himself. He was accompanied by Professor Blackie.

"Ha! So we have caught you, have we?" cried Professor Sharp, in tones of evident satisfaction. "Nice doings, these, for students of Brill. Aren't you ashamed of yourselves?" And he glared maliciously at the Rovers and Stanley Browne.

"Oh, Professor, can you—er—help us?" murmured Stanley. "We—er—are in a lot of trouble."

"So I see," answered Abner Sharp chillily. "Nice doings, I declare! Don't you think so?" he added to the other professor.

"It is too bad," murmured Professor Blackie. "I thought them all rather nice lads."

Dick's head was still dizzy, so he could not catch the import of the professor's words. He continued to work over Tom, who just then opened his eyes.

"Gi—give me a—a drink!" murmured poor Tom. His throat seemed to be on fire.

"Not another drop!" shouted Professor Sharp. "Not one! This is disgraceful! Look at what they have been drinking already!" And he pointed to the bottles scattered around.

"Say! What's the matter with you?" asked Sam, sleepily and angrily. He was doing his best to pull his wits together, and thus overcome the effects of the strange vapor.

"There is nothing the matter with me!" roared Professor Sharp. "The matter is with you, Rover. You have been drinking too much."

"Me? Drinking?" stammered Sam. "No, sir!"

"Rover, you may as well admit it," came from Professor Blackie. "It is a sad state of affairs."

"But I haven't been drinking."

"We know better. Look at the evidence!" roared Abner Sharp, pointing to the bottles. "Why, your very clothing smells of rum!" he added, smelling of Dick's shoulder.

"Sam has told you the truth. We haven't been drinking," said Dick.

"Rover, it would be better if you did not add falsehoods to your other shortcomings," said Professor Blackie. He was usually a very mild man, and had little to say outside of the classroom.

"You are mistaken," murmured Dick. It was all he could say, for he was still too bewildered to make a clear note of what was going on.

"This one seems to be the worst of all," said Abner Sharp, turning to Tom. "He must have drunk more than the others."

"He will have to sleep it off," answered Professor Blackie. "Too bad! Too bad! Why will young men do such things?" And he shook his head sorrowfully.

"I believe what the note said. This has been a regular hangout for the Rovers and their chums," said Professor Sharp severely. "It is high time it was broken up."

"Yes, yes," answered the other instructor. "How shall we—er—get them back to Brill?"

"I'll see about that. They must have some sort of a carriage here, or maybe somebody was going to call for them."

"Shall I take a look around?"

"If you will."

Professor Blackie looked around the house and grounds and then went through the tangle of a garden to the roadway. He espied Songbird coming along, driving the team rapidly and singing to himself. Songbird had passed an all-too-short hour with Minnie Sanderson.

"Stop, Powell!" cried the professor.

"I was going to, sir," answered the would-be poet cheerily. "How is this, Professor Blackie? Did you come to hunt for the ghost, too?"

"Ghost? I came for no ghosts—since there are no ghosts," was the quiet answer. "Were you to stop here?"

"Yes, sir, to pick up the three Rovers and Stanley Browne. They must be somewhere about. They came to explore the old house and to settle this ghost story."

"I think they came more for spirits than for ghosts," answered Professor Blackie dryly. "Then you know all about it, eh?"

"Why, yes."

"Then you knew they came here to drink and to carouse generally," went on the instructor, and his voice grew stern.

"Drink? Carouse? What are you talking about?" gasped Songbird. "The Rovers don't drink at all, and Stanley Browne drinks very little."

"Of course you wish to shield them, but it will do little good, Powell. Professor Sharp received word of what was going on, and he asked me to accompany him here. We have seen a sad sight. What Doctor Wallington will say when he hears of it, I cannot tell. I am afraid, however, that he will deal severely with the offenders."

"Professor Blackie, what you say is a riddle to me," answered Songbird. "I don't understand you at all."

"Then come with me, and perhaps you will understand," was the instructor's reply, and he led the way to the rear of the deserted house.

All of the students and Professor Sharp were now outside, on or near the back porch. Tom had recovered his senses, and Sam had obtained for him a drink of water from an old well. Much to the astonishment of the students, the professor had caught sight of a liquor flask in Tom's pocket, and had snatched it away.

"Here is evidence you cannot deny!" cried Abner Sharp in triumph. "All but empty, too!" he added, after shaking the flask and smelling of it.

"How did that—that get in m—my pocket?" mumbled poor Tom. He was still hazy in his mind.

"You probably know better than anybody else," retorted Professor Sharp. "And you can tell, too, where the liquor went to," he continued with a sneer.

"You're a—a—contemptible old sneak!" cried Tom wrathfully, "and if I didn't feel so—so dizzy I'd knock you down!"

"Tom!" cried Dick warningly. He was growing a little clearer in his mind, and could see that a terrible mistake had been made.

"You'll not knock anybody down, you young villain!" roared Abner Sharp in a rage. "I'll teach you to come here and drink and carouse, and bring disgrace upon the fair name of Brill College! I'll have you dismissed and sent home in disgrace!"

"You're making a mistake——" began Dick.

"No, there is no mistake. Of course you wish to hide the truth, and smooth matters over, but it won't go with me, nor with Professor Blackie, either," stormed Professor Sharp. "We know what we see and what we smell. You young fellows are a disgrace to Brill, and the sooner everybody knows it, the better. Now, then, march to the roadway, every one of you, and no more back talk!"

"But, sir——" began Stanley in dismay.

"Not another word!" cried Abner Sharp. "If you have anything more to tell, you may tell it to Doctor Wellington."

CHAPTER XXVII

IN DISGRACE

Still dizzy from the effects of the strange vapor, the students were driven rapidly over the country roads in the direction of Brill College. The fresh air served to make them feel a little better, but all were far from clear headed when ushered into the presence of Doctor Wallington.

"We have brought them back with us, sir," said Professor Sharp stiffly.

The president of the college gazed keenly at the Rovers and Stanley. They looked at him in return, but blinked and swayed as they did so.

"I will listen to the story," said Doctor Wallington, turning to the two instructors, and his voice had a hard tone to it that did not augur well for the students.

Thereupon Professor Sharp told how he had received an anonymous note stating that the Rovers and some others were going off to the old Jamison house to drink and gamble, and that it was thought they were going to take some innocent outsider with them, to fleece him of his money. On receiving the note Abner Sharp had called Professor Blackie into consultation with him, and had gone off, after leaving word for the doctor about what they proposed to do.

"We found them—the three Rovers and Stanley Browne—in a beastly state," continued Professor Sharp. "Truly beastly state—with empty liquor bottles and flasks strewn around, and Thomas Rover had a flask in his pocket, which I took from him." The instructor placed the flask on the president's desk. "There were also cigar butts scattered around, and some packs of playing-cards."

"Where was Powell?"

"He had dropped the others off at the old house and gone on to visit some folks named Sanderson. He came back later."

"Had he been drinking, too?"

"I do not think so," answered Professor Blackie.

During this talk Dick and his brothers and Stanley stared somewhat vacantly at the president and the professors. The students wanted to speak several times, but Doctor Wallington waved them to be silent.

"I will hear what you have to say after Professor Sharp and Professor Blackie have finished," said the head of the college.

He asked the instructors a great number of questions, and then turned to Dick, as the oldest of the boys.

"Now, then, what have you to say about your disgraceful conduct?" he demanded severely. "Or perhaps it would be as well to postpone further conversation until you are in a fit condition to tell a straight story." The doctor was sarcastic as well as severe.

"I—I am not well, sir," said Dick in a low voice. "None of us are. But it was not liquor that did it. It was the vapor."

"Vapor?" queried Doctor Wallington in perplexity.

"Yes, sir."

"What do you suppose he means?" and now the master of the college turned to Abner Sharp.

"When we found them in such a sad state they tried to excuse themselves by stating that a strange vapor had made them sick," was the instructor's reply. "But we could not trace any such vapor. I feel sure it is merely an excuse."

"You ought to have your head punched!" growled Tom. He was still sick, and the sickness made him reckless.

"Rover! How dare you?" exclaimed Doctor Wallington severely.

"I don't care! He is down on us, me especially, and he wants to put us in disgrace. He's a miserable sneak, that's what he is!"

"You are evidently in no condition to tell your story, and your companions are little better off," went on the head of the college. He turned to the two professors. "You may take them up to rooms 77 and 78, Mr. Blackie. I will confer with you further, Mr. Sharp."

There was no help for it, and with their heads still in a whirl, the Rovers and Stanley were taken to two rooms not used by any of the other students. The rooms were in an angle of the building, away from all others. They had a small hallway of their own, with a door shutting it off from the main hall.

Professor Blackie marched the boys into the rooms, and saw to it that they had a pitcher of fresh drinking water.

"You will have to remain here until Doctor Wallington sends for you," said the instructor, and walked out of the room. The boys heard him pass through the little hall and close and lock the door to the main hall.

"Prisoners! What do you think of that?" cried Sam.

"It is carrying matters with a high hand," answered Dick. He placed a hand on his forehead. "How my head aches!"

"Same here," answered Stanley. "I am going to rest," he added, and threw himself on one of the beds.

The others were glad to rest, also, and soon all were occupying the beds the connecting rooms contained. They left the windows wide open, so that they might get all the fresh air possible. Strange to say, each was soon in a profound slumber.

While they were sleeping they did not know that Professor Sharp came in to see if they wanted any supper. Seeing them sleeping so soundly, he notified Doctor Wallington.

"Do not disturb them," said the president of Brill. "Sleep will do them more good than anything. I doubt if they care to eat." And he heaved a sigh as he thought of the problem before him. He liked the Rovers and Stanley Browne, but according to what he had seen and been told, some of the strictest rules of Brill had been violated, and it would be impossible for him to pass the affair by or mete out ordinary punishment.

"I am afraid I shall have to dismiss them," he told himself. "Too bad!"

In some manner the story leaked out, and by Sunday noon all the students at Brill knew that the Rovers and Stanley were in disgrace, and in danger of dismissal. A few sided with the boys, but the majority shook their heads.

"They had no business to go off on such a lark," said one of the seniors. "It's a disgrace to the whole college. If they are sent home it will serve them right."

Koswell and Larkspur were in high glee over the success of their plot, and when alone winked at each other and poked each other in the ribs.

"They'll get what's coming to 'em this trip," said Bart Larkspur with a chuckle. "They'll be lucky if they are not sent home."

"And we'll rub it in, too," added Koswell. "You know how those Rovers are dead stuck on those girls at Hope."

"Sure."

"Well, I'll fix it so those girls hear all about this affair."

"Good!" cried Larkspur. "That will be the bitterest dose of all."

"Say," put in Dudd Flockley nervously, "you don't suppose there is any danger of our being found out?"

"Not the slightest," answered Koswell. "I saw to it that all our tracks were covered."

"But that fellow Parwick? Are you certain he can be trusted?"

"Yes. But we have got to pay him for his trouble. I promised him twenty dollars. I'll give him half and you can give him the other half," answered Koswell. He knew Larkspur had no spending money.

"Oh, I'm willing to pay him his price," said the dudish student. "But I want to be dead certain that he will keep his mouth shut."

"I'll make him do that," returned Jerry Koswell.

CHAPTER XXVIII

DARK DAYS

The Rovers and Stanley Browne were kept in the rooms until Monday morning. During that time their meals were sent to them, and Professor Sharp came to see them twice.

"Doctor Wellington will dispose of your case on Monday," said the instructor.

"I think we should have had a doctor," said Dick. "All of us were sick, and needed medical attention."

"Nonsense!" cried Abner Sharp. "You have sobered up, and that was all that was needed."

This assertion led to a war of words, and Tom came close to whacking the unreasonable teacher over the head with the water pitcher. As a consequence, Abner Sharp ran out of the room in fear and reported to the head of the institution that he had been assaulted.

On Monday morning the four boys were told to go down and report at the president's office. Previous to this they had held a "council of war," as Sam expressed it, and made Dick their spokesman.

"Now, then, as you appear to be sober, I will listen to your story," said Doctor Wallington. He was the only other person present. "And remember," he added sharply, "I want nothing but the truth. You cannot hope for any leniency on my part unless you tell me everything."

"That is what we propose to do, sir," answered Dick, looking the doctor full in the eyes. "My brothers and Stanley have asked me to do the talking for all of us. Shall I tell my story now?"

"Yes."

Thereupon Dick told his tale from beginning to end, very much as I have set it down here. He, of course, could tell nothing of the actions of Koswell and his crowd, for he had been unconscious most of the time.

"Certainly a remarkable story," mused Doctor Wallington, when the oldest Rover had finished. "And you mean to say you did not drink any of the liquor?"

"Not a drop, sir; and neither did the others."

"And this vapor? What was it, and how do you account for it?" The doctor's tones were very sceptical.

"I can't account for it, excepting by thinking it was part of a plot against us."

"Hum!" The doctor turned to Stanley. "Have you anything to add to Rover's story?"

"Nothing, sir, excepting that it is absolutely true, Doctor Wallington."

After this the boys were questioned for the best part of an hour, but without shaking their testimony in the least. Then Songbird was called in, and he told what he knew.

"If your story is true, it is a most extraordinary occurrence," said the head of Brill at last. "But I must confess that I can scarcely credit such a tale. However, I will, for the time being, give you the benefit of the doubt, and in the meantime make some investigations on my own account. If I find you have not told the truth I shall dismiss you from the college. Do you understand that?"

To this the students bowed.

"One thing more. All of you may return to your classes but Thomas Rover. He has an extra charge against him, that of assaulting Professor Sharp. Thomas Rover, you will remain here. The rest of you can go."

With strange feelings in their hearts Dick, Sam and Stanley, accompanied by Songbird, left the office. They had been heard, but had not been believed.

"We may be dismissed from here, after all," said Sam bitterly.

"What a shame!" cried Songbird. "Oh, if you could only find out who did it, and expose them!"

The boys went back to their classes with heavy hearts. They saw a number of the other students looking at them questioningly.

Jerry Koswell saw them return, and was much astonished. Had his plot to put them in disgrace miscarried, after all? Larkspur, too, was perplexed. Flockley was a bit relieved, and half hoped the whole matter would blow over and nothing more be heard of it.

The day went by, and the other lads did not see Tom. But they saw him in the evening, just before supper.

"Well, how did you make out?" asked Dick eagerly.

"Got a vacation," was Tom's laconic answer.

"Dismissed?" asked the others in concert.

"No, suspended until Doctor Wallington can investigate the whole matter more thoroughly. He wanted me to apologize to Sharp, and I said flatly that I wouldn't do it, because I hadn't anything to apologize for. He got mad at first, and threatened me with instant dismissal. Then I warmed up, and said I was innocent of all wrongdoing, and perhaps I'd be able to prove it some day, and if so, and I was dismissed, I'd sue the college for loss of reputation. That brought matters to a head, and I guess the doctor saw I was in deadly earnest. He told me I could consider myself suspended for two weeks, or until he could get to the bottom of the affair. So I've got a holiday."

"I'm glad you didn't apologize to Sharp," said Sam.

"What are you going to do with yourself—go home?" asked Dick.

"No. I am going to move to Ashton, and then try to get to the bottom of this matter."

"The doctor will send a letter home."

"So will I, and you must do the same. I think father will believe us."

Tom left that night, and established himself at the leading hotel in Ashton.

News travels swiftly, and Koswell and his cohorts took care that the girls at Hope should hear the story about the Rovers and Stanley and their supposed disgraceful doings. Dora, Nellie and Grace could scarcely believe their ears when they heard it.

"This is awful!" murmured Dora, and the tears came to her eyes.

"I don't believe one word of it!" cried Nellie with spirit.

"But Tom has been suspended," said Grace. "And think of poor Sam and Dick!" And her heart sank like lead within her bosom.

"I am going to send Dick a note right away," said Dora. "I cannot bear this suspense."

"But you don't think Dick is guilty, do you?" asked Nellie.

"No. But—but the disgrace! It is terrible!" And now Dora burst out crying in earnest.

The note from Dora reached Dick the following day, in the afternoon mail. It was short, but to the point, reading as follows:

"Dear Dick: We have just heard something awful about you and Tom and Sam. Tell us what it means. Of course we don't believe you have done anything wrong. "Yours,

"Dora."

This note disturbed Dick and Sam greatly, for they could understand how the evil report concerning them had been circulated at Hope Seminary, and how the girls had suffered in consequence.

"I am glad they think we are innocent," said Sam.

"They couldn't do anything else, knowing us as they do," returned his brother. And then he sent a note back stating that the reports were all falsehoods, and asking them to meet Tom and themselves on the following Saturday at Ashton.

"Perhaps Tom will have something to report by that time," said Dick.

The time to Saturday dragged miserably. The boys could not set their minds on their lessons, and as a consequence got some poor marks. For this Professor Blackie gave them a lecture.

"You ought to show your appreciation of what Doctor Wallington has done in your case," said the instructor.

"We can't settle down to lessons with this cloud hanging over us," answered Dick frankly. "It has got to be cleared away, or——" he did not finish.

"Or what, Rover?"

"Or I'm afraid we'll have to leave, even if we are not dismissed," was the slow answer, and Dick breathed a deep sigh.

WHAT THE GIRLS DISCOVERED

The Rover boys sent letters to their father, and on Saturday morning came replies from Mr. Rover. He said he was both surprised and shocked at what had occurred, and added that if they needed his aid he would come on at once. He showed that he believed them innocent, for which they were thankful.

"Here is more news," said Dick. "The case of Tad Sobber against the Stanhopes and the Lanings comes up in court next Tuesday; that is, they are going to argue the question of the injunction on that day."

"That will make Mrs. Stanhope and Mrs. Laning very anxious."

"Yes, and the girls, too, Sam."

"Well, we are anxious, too. Oh, I do hope our side wins!" cried Sam wistfully. "It would set me wild to see Tad Sobber get all that money!"

Dick and Sam were to meet Tom in Ashton at three o'clock, and all hoped that the girls would come later. Stanley could not go, for he had a Latin composition to write.

When the Rovers reached the hotel in Ashjton they found Tom impatiently awaiting them. By the look on his face they knew he had something to tell.

"Come up to my room," he said, and led the way to the apartment, located on the second floor, front.

"You can sit by the window, Dick, and keep a lookout for the girls," said Sam.

"Yes, they'll be here in about an hour," said Tom. "They telephoned this morning."

"Well, what have you discovered anything?" demanded Dick impatiently.

"I think I am on the right track," answered Tom. "Let me tell you what I've done. In the first place, I visited the haunted house yesterday morning, and went through it from celtlar to garret."

"Alone?" queried Sam.

"Yes, alone. But I carried a pistol, and I had it ready for use, too."

"I don't blame you," murmured Dick. "And I guess you looked to see if the doors were open, too."

"I did, and smashed out several windows in the bargain. The first place I investigated was that fireplace, and in it I found this." And Tom held up a bit of white paper. On it was printed:

m B. Schlemp
uggist.
ain St.

"That is from a druggist," said Dick.

"Exactly. I figure out the name is William B. Schlemp, that he is a druggist, and that he is doing business at some number on Main Street," came from Tom. "But I figure out more than that."

"What?"

"The paper was crumpled up, and had in it a few grains of a gray powder. I set the powder on fire and got that strange vapor that almost strangled us."

"You did!" cried Sam. "Then that stuff came from that druggist beyond a doubt."

"So I figure it. But there is no druggist named Schlemp here," went on Tom, "and the druggist here doesn't know of such a fellow."

"I know what we can do," cried Dick. "Don't you remember, Dan Baxter said he had worked for a wholesale drug house? We can telegraph and ask him if he knows of this Schlemp."

"Then let us do it at once," said Tom. "I have his route—the one he said he was to follow."

A few minutes later the following message, was being flashed over the wires to Dan Baxter, then supposed to be located at Detroit:

"Send full name and address of Blank B. Schlemp, druggist, at once. Highly important.
"Thomas Rover,

"Ashton Hotel."

"That was about all I found at the haunted house that was important," said Tom after the message had gone. "But I've found out something here that may lead to something else of value."

"What is that?" questioned Sam.

"There is a fellow hanging around here named Henry Parwick. He is rather dissipated, and does not seem to work for a living. One night this Parwick had been drinking pretty freely, and he got into a quarrel with one of his companions. They taunted each other about money, and Parwick said he had some good friends up to Brill who would give him all the cash he wanted. The other fellow wanted to know that was, and Parwick winked one eye and answered, 'Oh, there's a reason, Buddy, a good reason. They wouldn't dare to refuse me.' Since that time I have seen Parwick talking to Jerry Koswell and Bart Larkspur."

"Do you think this Parwick helped Koswell and the others in a plot against us?" asked Dick.

"It may be so. Anyway, I think Parwick has some kind of a hold on Koswell, for I saw Jerry give him some money."

"This is certainly interesting," mused Dick. "Do you suppose we could corner this Parwick and get him to talk?"

"We might, but I have another plan."

"What is that?"

"To watch Parwick, and follow him when I think he is going to meet Koswell and the others. I may be able to overhear their talk."

"Good!"

After that Dick and Sam told Tom of what had occurred at the college since their brother had left Sam was just relating the particulars of a stormy interview with Professor Sharp when Dick uttered a cry.

"Look! Here comes Dora, and she is running!"

One after another the brothers ran down to the ground floor of the hotel and hurried outside.

"Oh, I am so glad I found you all together!" vried Dora, panting for breath. "Come quick"'

"Where to?" queried Dick.

"Down the road about half a mile. We just saw that Jerry Koswell and Bart Larkspur, and they are having a quarrel with a man who acts as if he was half intoxicated."

"It must be Henry Parwick!" ejaculated Tom.

"Yes, his name is Parwick," said Dora. "We heard Koswell mention it."

"Where are they?" asked Sam as the whole party hurried down the main street and out of Ashton, Dora leading the way.

"They are at a cottage where an old woman named Brice lives. We were going to stop for a drink of water when we heard voices, and saw the young men. Then Nellie and Grace heard them mention you, and they asked me to come here and get you just as quickly as possible. They sa4d they would remain, and, if possible, hear what it was all about."

"I think we are on the right track!" cried Dick joyfully. "Maybe matters will come to a head quicker than we imagined."

"Dick, you stay with Dora!" cried Tom. "Come on, Sam!" And off the two brothers sped at top speed, leaving Dick and Dora to follow as rapidly as the strength of the girl would permit.

Curiosity lent strength to the legs of the two Rovers, and they covered the distance to the Brice cottage in an incredibly short space of time. As they came into view they beheld Grace watching for them. She held up her hand for caution. She was standing in among some bushes by the roadside.

"Be careful, or those wicked boys will see you!" she cried in a low voice. "They are back of the cottage, near the barn."

"Where is Nellie?" asked Tom.

"She is watching them."

"Have you learned anything?" asked Sam.

"Yes, indeed. We have learned that Koswell, Larkspur and Flockley were guilty of this plot against you, and that a man named Parwick aided them by getting a strange powder for them, the powder that made you dizzy and sick," were Grace's words, and they filled th Rovers with much satisfaction.

A BEGINNING AND AN ENDING

"It was Allan Charter's coming that clinched matters," said Tom. "Doctor Wallington might not have believed us, but he had to believe Charter."

"He had to believe the girls, too," added Dick. "He knew they would not tell him such falsehoods. But I am glad Charter came along. He hated to get mixed up in it, I know, but he acted the man about it, didn't he?"

"Wonder what the doctor will do with Koswell & Company?" questioned Sam.

"Fire 'em, most likely, and they deserve tobe fired," growled Stanley. "Oh, when I think of the trick that was played I feel like wiping up the floor with every one of those scoundrels!"

"It was certainly a bit of dirty work," was Dick's comment.

The boys were seated in Sam and Tom's room, talking it over. It was Sunday afternoon, and outside the sun shone brightly and a light breeze stirred the trees.

It had proved a strenuous Saturday afternoon and evening. Dick and Dora had come up, meeting Allan Charter, the leading senior of Brill, on the way. They had persuaded Charter to accompany them to the Brice cottage, and there all had witnessed a bitter quarrel between Henry Parwick and Koswell, Larkspur and Flockley. Parwick was semi-intoxicated, and in a maudlin way had exposed all that had been done at the haunted house. He had spoken about getting the powder for them, and mentioned how Koswell had fixed a fuse and lit it, and he told of getting the liquor bottles and flasks and other things. He had warmed up -during his recital, and had demanded fifty dollars on the spot. When refused he had threatened to go to the Brill authorities and "blow everything." Then Koswell had threatened, if this was done, that he would have Parwick arrested for robbing his former employer, William Schlemp. Then had come blows, and in the midst of this Charter had stepped forward and confronted the evildoers.

"We have seen and heard all," he had said sternly. "I am a witness, and so are these young ladies. You, Koswell, Flockley and Larkspur, ought to be ashamed of yourselves. I never dreamed any students of Brill could be so bad. I shall report to Doctor Wallington without delay."

Charter had been as good as his word, and had been closeted with the head of the college for an hour. The girls went back with Tom, Dick and Sam, and also had an interview with the president. Then Doctor Wallington sent for Flockley, Koswell and Larkspur. Only Flockley answered the summons, and it was learned that Koswell and Larkspur were afraid to come back, fearing arrest. Parwick had also disappeared. Then had come a telegram from Dan Baxter giving the address of the druggist, Schlemp. Word was sent to this man, and later he wrote that Parwick had once worked for him, but had been discharged for drunkenness and because he was not honest.

The interview between Doctor Wallington and Flockley was a most affecting one. The dudish student broke down utterly, and confessed all. He said Koswell had hatched out the plot, aided by Larkspur, and that he himself had been a more or less unwilling participant. He told much about Parwick, and how that dissolute fellow had spoken of having the strange powder, which was a Japanese concoction, and which, if used often, would render a person insane. He begged the good doctor to forgive him and said he would be willing to do anything in order to remain at Brill.

"My father will never forgive me if I am dismissed," he said in a broken voice.

"But supposing I had dismissed the Rovers and Stanley Browne?" asked the doctor severely.

"Yes, yes, I know, sir!" wailed Flockley. "But, oh, sir, don't send me away! I'll do anything if you'll let me stay!"

"I will think it over," answered the head of Brill shortly. And thus Flockley was dismissed from the office.

"It was certainly a wicked piece of work," said Songbird to the others in the room. "I really think somebody ought to be arrested."

Tom was about to speak when a footstep sounded in the hall, and a knock on the door followed. Sam opened the portal, to behold Flockley standing there, hat in hand. The dudish student was as white as the wall, his clothing looked dishevelled, and his shoes were unblacked, a great contrast to the Flockley of old.

"What do you want?" asked Sam abruptly.

"I want—I want——" commenced Flockley brokenly. Then he stepped into the room and confronted Dick. "Oh, Rover!" he cried, "won't you—won't you please, please get Doctor Wallington to let me stay at Brill? Please don't let him send me home! I'll do anything—apologize, get down on my knees, if you like—but please help me to stay here!"

Flockley caught Dick by the arm and continued to plead, and then he entreated Sam, Tom, and Stanley, also. It was a truly affecting scene. They all commenced to speak. He had been so mean, wicked, so unlike a decent college fellow, how could they forgive him?

And then came a pause, and during that pause a distant church bell sounded out, full and clear, across the hills surrounding Brill. Dick listened, and so did his brothers and Stanley, and the anger in their faces died down.

"Well, I'm willing you should stay," said Dick, "and I'll speak to the doctor about it, if you wish."

"And so will I," added Sam and Tom, and Stanley nodded.

"But you ought to cut such fellows as Koswell and Larkspur," said Tom.

"I will! I will!" said Flockley earnestly.

The Rovers and Stanley Browne were as good as their word. On the following day they had another interview with the head of the college and spoke of Flockley.

"Well, if you desire it, he can remain," said Doctor Wallington. "As for Koswell and Larkspur, I doubt if they wish to return, since they have not yet shown themselves. You can prosecute them if you wish."

"No, we don't want to do that," said Dick. "We have talked it over, and we think, for the honor of Brill, the least said the better."

"That conclusion does you much credit, and I feel greatly relieved," said the head of the college. He turned to Tom. "You are, of course, reinstated, Thomas, and I shall see to it that the marks placed against your name are wiped out. I sincerely trust that you and Professor Sharp will allow bygones to be bygones, and will make a new beginning."

"I'm willing," answered Tom. And a little later he entered one of the classrooms and he and Professor Sharp shook hands. After school Professor Blackie came up and shook hands all around.

"I am glad to know you are exonerated," said that professor. "This has taught me a lesson, to take nothing for granted," he added.

When the truth became known many of the students flocked around the Rovers and Stanley and Songbird, and congratulated them on the outcome of the affair. Flockley did not show himself for a long time, excepting at meals and during class hours.

"He feels his position keenly," said Dick. "Well, I hope he turns over a new leaf."

"A telegram for Richard Rover," said one of the teachers to the boys a few days later.

""Wonder what's up now?" mused Dick as he tore open the yellow envelope. He read the slip inside. "Hurrah! This is the best news yet!" he cried.

"Vhat is it?" asked Tom and Sam.

"The injunction against the Stanhopes and the Lanings is dissolved by the court. They can keep the fortune. Tad Sobber has had his case thrown out of court!"

"Say, that's great!" ejaculated Tom, and in the fullness of his spirits he turned a handspring.

"I reckon that's the end of Mr. Tad Sobber," said Sam. But the youngest Rover was mistaken. Though beaten in court, Sobber did not give up all idea of gaining possession of the fortune, and what he did next will be related in another volume, to be called "The Rover Boys Down East; Or, The Struggle for the Stanhope Fortune." In that book we shall also meet Jerry Koswell and Bart Larkspur once more, and learn how they tried again to injure our friends.

But for the time being all went well, and the Rover boys were exceedingly happy. As soon as possible they met the girls, and all spent a happy half day in taking another ride in an automobile. From Flockley they gradually learned how Koswell and Larkspur had done many mean things, including putting the glass in the roadway, and using the pencil box out of Tom's dress-suit case.

"Vacation will soon be at hand," cried Sam one day, "and then——"

"We'll have the best time ever known," finished Tom.

"Ah, vacation time," put in Songbird. "I have composed some verses about that season. They run like this——"

"Not to-day, Songbird," interrupted Dick. "I've got to bone away at my geometry."

"Then hurry up, Dick," said Sam. "I want you to come and play ball."

"Ball it is—in half an hour," answered Dick. "And then," he added softly to himself, "then I, guess I'll write a good long letter to Dora."

THE END

CPSIA information can be obtained
at www.ICGtesting.com
Printed in the USA
BVHW011821140319
542697BV00002B/92/P

9 781540 762818